ANGELS AND WITCHESS

ANGELS AND WITCHESS

ROBERTA BAUM

ANGELS and WITCHESS is a work of fiction.
Names, characters, places and incidents either are the product of the author's imagination or are used fictitiously. Any resemblance to actual persons, living or dead, events and locales is entirely coincidental.

Copyright @2025 by Roberta Baum
All Rights Reserved

Published by Prunella Publishing / March 2025

No part of this book may be reproduced in any manner what so ever or transmitted in any form or by any means, electronic or mechanical, including photocopying, recording or by any information storage and retrieval system without written permission by the publisher.

Library of Congress Cataloging in Publication Data
Names: Baum, Roberta, author

Title: Angels and Witchess / Roberta Baum
Description: First Edition/ Prunella Publishing [2025]

Identifiers:
ISBN 979-8-9883611-0-7 Hardcover Print
ISBN 979-8-9883611-1-4 E book
ISBN 979-8-9883611-2-1 Paperback

Subjects:
 1. Visionary Fiction 2. New York City 3. Angels 4. Romance 6. Botanical Fantasy

First Edition
Book Design by Roberta Baum
Front Cover Photo by Quang-Nguyen-Vinh

For
Tarleton

1

Falling, Falling, Falling

When the first one appeared no one took notice. No one was there to see her fall. She fell so softly, born on the wind into the snow. Cold she did not feel. But heavy she did. Her wings were soaking wet. So unnatural to her. Only the beauty of the snow tempered the shock of their weight.

People were still sleeping far down the mountainside, as more of the Angels arrived. Cascading luminous streaks across every horizon. Orbs of light morphing into human form.

First flesh and bone, then denser harder heavier than stone. Each one an exquisite work of art. Some were seven, some were eight, some almost nine feet tall. Without hunger, without thirst. Soon their bodies would be completely paralyzed except for their eyes. Their eyes would remain sentient. Brimming with wonder, reveling in the blessing of movement.

This was so unexpected. Such a jarring break from eternity. No warning. No explanation. They begin consoling one another.

"This must be a plan from on high."

"Yes, of course it is God's plan."

"We will wait. We will trust. We must."

2

New Witch, New York

Whenever electric storms threaten to strike the bedrock of Manhattan Isle, Euphoria Green goes rushing out onto her balcony to catch the first bolt just before it hits the ground.

Flinging her arms wide apart, palms open and ready to receive the lightening juice. One good crash zigzagging across the darkened sky is all it takes. Like the Bride of Frankenstein, Euphoria's midnight blue hair shoots vertically up into the air. Her veins begin pulsing with brilliant crimson light.

"One Two Three," she counts, releasing her arms to let the storm resume its course. Removing her nightgown she chants in a low childish whisper,

"This is how we Witchess wake. Wake from sleep, sweet and deep. To charge our blood with celestial fire, then bath in moonlight silvered water."

Euphoria's bed chamber is a grand and spacious event. There are several adjoining rooms that can only be accessed behind cleverly hidden doors. Opening one now she descends seven shallow stone steps into a steaming teal blue hot spring pool.

Fresh bees wax candles are flickering softly in deep wall niches, casting a pale golden light. Euphoria dives into the pool like a frog, submerging her whole body in its warm soothing waters. Then flipping over for a few backstrokes, she speaks to the air.

"I know you stones have ears, so listen well and hear my heart. I need enemies. I need conflict. I need jealousy. I crave competition."

Floating on her back she waits for a response.
Finally one stone hisses,
"Drama Queen."

"Is that so? Well, perhaps you are right, I am a Drama Queen. Drama Queen For A Day," she says sadly.

Unlike those women living on Manhattan Isle, who will go dancing round the May Pole today, Euphoria Green will not be joining them. Fertility is not her concern. Finding a mate for her, is a lost art. Who can blame her? There's only so much one can do whilst living a double life, as she does. Instead, she has perfected the art of sublimation. Transposing her feral instincts for intimacy and union with a man into a rapturous love affair with Nature.

Emerging from the hot spring pool, Euphoria takes a stand against the wisps of self pity gathering in her breast.

"Witchess do not practice Magic. Witchess are Magic. I will dazzle everyone today wearing my pale violet silk mini dress, deep violet fish net stockings and my soft as butter ox blood leather boots. I can certainly indulge a bit while pretending to be an ordinary witch for a few hours with some blue Lapis eye shadow, black kohl eye liner, dark blue mascara and this utterly gorgeous violet lip gloss." Euphoria goes to work transforming her visage.

While New Witch, New York maybe in this world, it is not of this world. Preternatural events brought Euphoria's ancestors across its threshold to safety, giving them sanctuary from death and destruction to their way of life. Having both Lenape and

Dutch ancestry has given Euphoria bold facial features, that often times clash. Large hooded sapphire eyes with thick black eyebrows. A sardonic sensual mouth and a long prominent nose equipped with high flaring nostrils. Intimidating perhaps, but excellent shape for distinguishing between the cacophony of fragrances permeating the Enchantment Garden.

Opening her jewelry box Euphoria chooses her great-great-great-grandmother Arabella's rosary. Made in Amsterdam and brought to the New World by Arabella's family in the early 1600's. Rubies and rose quartz beads on a chain of tiny gold florets featuring a gold double locket. Inside the locket there are two hand painted enamel portraits, one is of the Virgin Mary and the other is of Jesus. Holding the locket with both hands she prays.

"Mother Mary, Undoer Of Knots, dissolve all discord gathering in my heart. Your plan is always better than mine, Amen."

Attaching two pouches of powdered gem stones to a utility belt slung low on her hips, she is ready for her morning Sigil flight. Stepping out on the balcony, she leaps off its edge and disappears into the pale mists of dawn.

3

Euphoria's Sigil Flight

Boundaries between New Witch and Manhattan Isle expand and recede like puddles in the rain. If you are standing on Riverside Drive and 122nd Street and throw your head back, you will see the sky and tops of trees and perhaps some clouds. But what you will not see, is Euphoria Green leaping off her balcony.

You'll miss her slow descent onto the skyline of Manhattan Isle. Not a fast moving streak across the sky, but drifting like a cloud, to fully savor the scent she loves of the city below. You'll miss her graceful gliding like that of a mast head carving upon an ancient ship. Steering her course with only a twist of a wrist, or angle of an ankle. You will not see the whorls of powdered crystals scattering to streets below, as she pulls them by handfuls from the pouches attached to her belt. Though perhaps later you will see a rooftop or sidewalk glittering in the moonlight.

"What a strange dawn. Ghostly gray for May. What is this? Huge feathery flakes of snow are falling. I'll have to carve my Sigil into their path, twist the E and G sharper and tighter through the center," Euphoria whispers to herself.

Gliding over Central Park, letting her hands run through the tops of the trees, Euphoria is intoxicated by the scent of cherry blossoms and snow flakes melting on her tongue. She loops a knot high above Bethesda fountain and heads further east, then south again along 5th Avenue towards the river.

"Above Brooklyn Bridge something catches my eye. Too bright for this pale gray sky, too large for a snowflake. It is a streak descending in an arc towards Lady Liberty's torch.

I decide to veer off my flight's path and get closer to see what it is. The streak has congealed into an oblong orb of light. Then begins morphing into the shape of a man. At first he is translucent, then golden bronze. His features continue redefining themselves, receding back and forth, as if he cannot make up his mind. Finally they come to rest. He is lean yet muscular, with long ebony hair and enormous opalescent wings. An absolutely spectacular male specimen, so I move in as close as I dare."

"I am who you choose to see," he says.

His voice goes through me like two warm hands caressing my spine.

My legs go limp. I spill his name.

"Adore," I gush.

"Closer," Adore says.

I am Smashed.

"Adore," He repeats pulling me like a magnet.

"Oh No," I gasp in pure terror as I see his flesh is turning hard, solid, shiny, not human at all. His face has gone completely rigid except for his eyes. They are still liquid pools of golden light, emanating mysterious strength and emotion.

Horrified I protest.

"No, too close, stop."

But it's too late.

The instant our eyes meet, there is such a deep recognition between us. I hear a deafening roar. Then a sudden blast.

All goes black.

***

Next thing I remember, is waking up on the grass at the base of Lady Liberty.

"Dear God, what just happened?"

Looking up, I see Adore is still perched upon the Lady's torch.

"I will hold back," Adore explains.

Still shaken, I get up, brush myself off inhaling deeply to regain my equilibrium.

"OK… You do that. I'm late for work," I say trying to be polite.

Wobbling like a duck, Euphoria rises into the air, away from Adore as fast as she can.

She heads north, back uptown, where her brother Glorious is waiting for her at Faery Cakes Bakery Cafe on Broadway and La Salle Street.

4

Faery Cakes Bakery Cafe

It is 6:00 am and lights are on inside Faery Cakes Bakery Cafe. Glorious Green, in his vintage baker's apron made of mustard colored oil cloth is baking savory Faery Pies while whisking fruits, berries and spices for today's Flower Soup Specials. Local college students will soon be forming a line outside when the Bakery Cafe opens its doors for breakfast at 8:00 am.

Faery Cakes is old school. Nothing digital and no wi-fi. With gas lit ovens and stove tops, vintage refrigerators and real linoleum floors. The kitchen boasts a huge skylight, so there's plenty of sunlight and starlight for the staff to work by.

Inside the Bakery are cedar wood counters with mulled glass cased shelves. Perfect for showing off fresh sprouted grain breads, their signature Faery Cake pies, heavenly cupcakes and the much adored fruit & nut bars.

The Cafe tables are all made from round white pine slabs with tree trunk pedestals. In contrast chairs are vintage Lucite shells, that swivel and are easy to move as students gather in groups or disperse to study. A ceiling fan made of amber resin studded with rhinestones, spins slowly making tiny rainbows in the air.

A forest landscape graces the Cafe walls that changes with the seasons in subtle, incremental steps. Patrons are at a loss as to how this happens, yet secretly thrilled to remain within the mystery of such crafty delight. No one dares ask how.

Ingredients for all of Faery Cakes menu comes straight from the Enchantment Garden in New Witch. Glorious and Euphoria maintain their secret cover by keeping their produce in crates and sacks and jars that have labels from organic farms in the Hudson Valley. That is how they can justify the over the top quality of their menu offerings and herbal apothecary.

Faery Cakes Magic abounds especially when it comes to honey. Glorious is beesotted with all things Bee. Bee Propolis, Bee Pollen, Royal Jelly, Bees wax, in various combinations for medicinal and edible purposes. He and his Grandmother Promise have created Gemstone Honey, the most magnificent honey on earth. Dazzling special effects are produced by infusing Hibiscus tea with Topaz Honey, as it bursts into an flaming Orange sunset in your cup. Or Elderberry tea with Sapphire Honey that suddenly explodes into an Indigo sky with falling stars.

In the corner of the Bakery is a little nook Apothecary where Euphoria offers her herbal teas and tinctures. The ongoing buzz among women in the local community has created a demand for her Herbal Wisdom class Sunday mornings.

5

Euphoria Tells Glorious

Euphoria wobbles into Faery Cakes kitchen over an hour late. Glorious looks her up and down.

"What happened to you?" he asks.

Her dress is grass stained and terribly creased. Her fishnet stockings are torn in several places and her hair is a total mess.

"You won't believe me even if I tell you," she whimpers.

"Try me," Glorious whimpers back at her

Euphoria leans in close to her brother's face,

"I was smashed by an Angel."

"I take it that means, you met a guy," Glorious says smirking.

"Met is not exactly what I'd call it. I promise I'll share details with you later." Euphoria begins shimming.

Glorious eyes light up with enjoyment.

"Should I get Myra to cover for you?"

"No, not at all, I'm just a little wobbly. Actually, I feel really, really good. All I need right now is a cup of Cacao Rose Pudding and I'll be good to go," Euphoria licks her lips, undulating her torso.

Glorious imitates her.

"Oh yeah, you are feeling good."

Euphoria's laughter says it all and bang, a Circle of Stars starts rotating clockwise inside her sapphire eyes, a Witchess response to pleasure. Concealing this reaction though is a constant challenge at work.

Faery Cakes patrons and friends regard Euphoria and Glorious as a wee bit over the top theatrical, but otherwise just your typical, lovable, eccentric, witchy New Yorkers.

Alas, these two bonafide Witchess have to play pretend Witches on a daily basis. Lots of glam glitter eye shadow and tinted eye glasses are always on hand to conceal their weird wonderful spinning Circle of Stars eyes.

"I'm being interviewed for a foodie magazine today, so keep your eyes calm OK?" Glorious adds with a wink.

Faery
Deserts First

* Rose Cacao Pudding *
Hemp Milk, Raw Cacao, Rose Water, Monk Fruit
topped with Rose Petals and crushed Pistachio Nuts

* Violet Ice Cream *
Fresh Violets, Coconut Cream, Violet Honey & Crystal Ginger
Surrounded by edible Violets and fresh Raspberries

* Pansy Pie *
Almond Flour Pie Crust filled with Coconut Orange Pudding
topped with Fresh Edible Pansies and crushed Walnuts

* Date Nut Roll *
Dried Dates, Pecans, Coconut flakes and Cardamon Seeds
served with Fresh Black Cherry dipping Sauce

* Bittersweet Cacao Pie *
Macadamian Nut Milk, Raw Cacao & Rose Honey,
Topped with Walnuts & Bittersweet Chocolate Flakes
served with Fresh Orange Slices and Fresh Nasturtiums

* Poppy Seed Cookies *
Almond & Bucketwheat Flour, Monk Fruit, Coconut Oil, Flax Seeds
served with Fresh Figs and Fresh Lilacs

Cakes

Flower Soups

* Blueberry Soup *
Fresh Blueberries, Apricot Nectar,
Fresh Pomegranate Juice and Violet Honey and Pansies
Served with Fig Kiwi Toast

* Watermelon Gumbo *
Made with Fresh Watermelon Rosettes, Kiwi slices,
Fresh Strawberries, Fresh Pineapple and Sage Flowers
Served with Pecan Nut Bread

Faery Pies

* Faery Bean Pie *
Buckwheat Flour Pie Crust
Filled with Aduki Beans, Water Chestnuts
Sweet Green Peas & Maitake Mushrooms
Served with Fresh Spinach & Heirloom Tomatoes w/Basil Vinagrette

* Faery Shroom Pie *
Chick Pea Flour Pie Crust
Filled with Maitake, Lions Mane, Oyster, Cordecepts & Shitake Mushrooms,
Steamed Carrots, Scallions, Celery & Dulse strips
Served with Alfalfa Sprouts, Cucumber, Fresh Dill & Mint Leaves

6

Glorious Green

Glorious Green, of raven hair and sapphire eyes, smash both sexes to pieces. Wearing his long thick mane like a Lenape warrior in a single braid down his back, Glorious thrives whilst creating mouth watering edibles in the kitchen. Although he has many admirers at Faery Cakes, some students literally swooning at his feet, having an intimate relationship has always been more problematic than pleasurable.

"They don't really see me. All they see is a beautiful prize they want to win and own," Glorious confides to Grandmother Promise when she asks if he's dating anyone.

Glorious tries in vain to look nerdy in baggy yoga pants and loose T shirts. Little does he realize his lithe limbs, dancing beneath folds of draped fabric scream out even more sensuality to anyone looking. The spirit of Nijinsky lives inside Glorious, as he leaps and pirouettes along Riverside Drive.

Raised by their Grandmother after their mother, Peace Green died, both Glorious and Euphoria suffer terribly when it comes to intimacy and romance. Unlike Grandmother Promise who can still revel in ecstatic encounters at 156. Go figure.

7

Glorious Magazine Interview

Glorious one long standing love affair has been with food. His hands are a force to be reckoned with when it comes to handling produce. He fondles their bodies, caresses their skin, massages their flesh; we're talking fruits here, we're talking plucked right out of the soil, brazen and bold veggies, rippling ripe grains, weird ass alien fungi, bewitched and bejeweled legumes, hypnotic herbs, exotic spices and oozing oils.

Reporter Jasper Ray is there to interview Glorious Green for a local foodie Magazine called Taste Buds.

Sitting across from him at the Cafe, Jasper hits the record button on his audio recorder.

"So tell me Glorious, what inspired you to become a baker?"

Glorious eyes light up, remembering the look on his mother's face when he made his first Smoothie.

"As a child I was totally fascinated by Smoothies. Blending different things, mixing them all together, knowing I could create an entire meal in one drink excited me. After that I got hooked on making soup. That's when my mother knew when I was ready to learn about herbs and flowers. She taught me which flowers were edible and which herbs were good for healing. At a very young age, I already understood that Food is Medicine."

Glorious pauses, hoping that Jasper will grasp the importance of what he has just said.

Unfortunately Jasper seems to have missed the point.

"Right. So when did you start baking?"

"I loved watching my Grandmother bake and I saw that baking is just like making a smoothie with one more step. You put what you blend into the oven. By the time I was ten, I knew I wanted to have my own Bakery."

Glorious jumps up and grabs a Faery Cake menu. Handing it to Jasper, he bows,

"Order anything you like, it's on the house," he says.

"Wow, thank you," Jasper says, opening the menu.

"This looks amazing," Jasper calls out.

"Glorious, one more question. Why is the Dessert section at the top of your menu?"

Glorious spins back around and explains.

"We always do desserts first back home. Tiny portions of course. Nothing like starting off a meal with a tea cup of raw cacao pudding or a tiny oozing fruit pie or some mouth watering shredded nut meats rolled in ginger, honey and coconut to get your digestive juices flowing."

Jasper starts salivating.

"Well now, you've just gone got my digestive juices flowing."

8

Euphoria Basks

"I do not want this day to end," Euphoria prays while returning to New Witch later that afternoon.

"I want to savor my encounter with Adore, my body is still buzzing from that moment before I blacked out. What was that between us? What kind of Angel has that power? Did it happen because we were together?

Feeling her knees starting to buckle, afraid she'll swoon again, she lands in the Enchantment Garden and lies down on the grass, surrendering her weight to the warm earth, inhaling slowly.

"We didn't even touch. Just by looking into his eyes."

She imagines Adore holding her, his body pinning her down. She cannot move a single finger. Her tailbone starts throbbing. Desire spreading fast up into her loins, then further along her spine. Suddenly she hears that deafening roaring sound again, like a tornado heading her way. Only this time Euphoria does not black out. She rides it. Rides over and beyond it, until it subsides on its own.

Rocking back and forth on the grass, laughing hysterically,

"Oh no. No, no, no. Oh God. I'm falling in love with an Angel."

9

Euphoria Returns To Lady Liberty

Unable to sleep, Euphoria returns to Lady Liberty in the hope of seeing Adore again.
"There he is," she exhales in relief.

She hovers several feet away off to the side of him, looking straight ahead so as not to meet his eyes. In the moonlight his opalescent wings make an inviting alcove. But the thought of being that close to him makes her too nervous. Her body, still humming from this morning's encounter makes the stillness between them unbearable.

She finally brakes the silence and gets straight to the point.
"What happened this morning?
Adore does not respond.
"What happened between us?
"I am who you choose to see," Adore says.
Euphoria's heart begins to sink.
"What happened between us, is still happening inside me. Is it still happening inside you?"

"I am who you choose me to be," Adore says.

"Are you saying that I decide how you are feeling?"

"Yes, you decide," Adore confirms.

"Do you feel anything on your own?"

"I feel everything. Nothing is mine to own," Adore explains.

"So, it does not matter if it is me. It could be anyone and you would say the same thing?" Euphoria says, crushed.

"Yes, the same thing would be told," Adore confirms.

With that, Euphoria bolts up into the air and flies off in a shrieking fit. There are bright red sparks shooting out from her hair leaving a trail of smoke behind her.

10

Euphoria Retreats To New Witch Forest

Euphoria is fuming all the way back to New Witch. Shaking with rage in a torrential rant, she heads into the forest.

"Why would I ever choose him? A totally unfeeling, untouchable, unavailable, unattainable frozen gargoyle. He's not a real man. A real living man I can be myself with. I never meet anyone like that. What was that that happened between us? So powerful that I actually blacked out from it?

And now, now I feel more alive than I ever have in my entire life. Every cell of me is still buzzing with it."

Kneeling down at the foot of an ancient Oak tree.

"Mother Oak, How will I survive after looking into those eyes? I needed to hear him say yes, yes Euphoria, its you. Isn't that what love is? Isn't love a choice?"

Euphoria goes face down, weeping into the moss.

"Mother, please take me down now. I' am sick from too much desire, too weak from the memory of him. If this is Love, then it acts as poison upon my soul. Mother take me under and let me hide, let me heal in the earth between your roots,"

Mother Oak yields and yawns deep from below the base of her trunk. The earth parts and swallows Euphoria's entire body. Then just as quickly the earth closes up over her again.

No one will ever suspect, that lying beneath this mound of moss, Euphoria is coiled like a shell....

11

Grandmother Promise

Grandmother Promise has traveled around the Sun for over one hundred and fifty-six years. With so many lifetimes rolled into one, she revels going incognito these days and has taken New York's female senior population by a storm with her podcast series, *Clitasaurus - Dinosaur Priestess Talk Show Hostess*. Under her provocative persona, Promise Green defies today's prevalent youth cult obsession. As Clitasaurus she guides senior women to an entirely new realm. Without any New Age retreats, Goddess worshiping or Tantric yoga, she reveals the real craft of a Crone is pure self activation. As Clitasaurus says,

"It's always an inside job."

This morning Clitasaurus is in her Tribeca studio, seated upon her throne. A high back cerulean blue velvet Victorian chair. Her long pale blond Chamomile infused hair is piled high upon her head in a style centuries old. Wearing a turquoise silk kaftan, coral silk pants and adorned with a lapis bead choker, lapis earrings and numerous enormous gemstone rings.

Straightening her spine, her bra-less, pendulous breasts still afloat, she leans forward flipping her studio microphone switch to

ON and begins speaking in her croaking slightly in a raspy contralto register,

"Good morning my lovelies!! I have a surprise for you today. The theme for this month's podcast series is....."

She raps her fingers like a drum roll on her desk top.

"*Are You Vagina Mindful?*" That's right. You heard me right, ladies. "*Are You Vagina Mindful?*" Mind Fullness dropping down, down, down. From between your ears to between your legs." Clitasaurus checks her computer screen to see what kind of response her announcement is getting. The chat box is filling up fast with affirmative emojis and comments.

Satisfied, she continues. "Did you know my lovelies, that your Vagina is your whole self? It is your eyes, your feet. It moves with you everywhere you go. It sees everything you look at, tastes everything you eat, it hears every word you speak. It sleeps with you every night and sits with you all day long, every day, every year. Your Vagina shares your life with you for better or for worse, in sickness and in health, till Death do you part. No man will ever be as close, will ever know your heart as well as your Vagina. Vagina is so much more than a hot throbbing pleasure vortex. Vagina is where you accept or reject, people, places, thoughts, situations, whether you realize it or not. It is she who chooses to initiate or retreat. She is the captain of your ship. She pulls the strings, focuses the lens, turns the ignition on, pushes the gas pedal and applies the brakes." Clitasaurus pauses to take a sip of water from her Bavarian crystal chalice.

"So my lovelies, I ask you, Are You Vagina Mindful?"

Questions and comments are pouring in like crazy. The program is in full swing for the next hour and a half.

Clitasaurus is on a roll...

12

Promise Meets Onyx

After her morning podcast Clitasaurus goes back to being Promise Green again. Letting her hair down she goes up to the roof to bask in the sunshine and unwind from all the excitement her show has stirred up.

Behold, a vision of supreme splendor is standing on the roof's skylight dome. An Angel in a sheer sparkling gown. Her eyes are as gold as a cat. Her skin is ebony black. Flecks of gold catching sunlight in her plum coiled hair. With shimmering Topaz wings and head dress glittering with gold stars, that make Promise think of the 1920s silent film star, Theda Bara.

Promise holds her breath and kneels at the Angel's feet waiting for some sign, some explanation, wondering if this is the beginning of a flash mob event. She waits a few more minutes, then finally breaks the ice by singing

"You'll Never Get Too Heaven If You Break My Heart."

As if on cue, the Angel finally speaks.

"I am who you choose to see," she says.

Her voice is so rich, so cool, so musical. Promise is delighted.

"Am I who you choose to see?" Promise asks hopefully.

"I cannot say," The Angel says.

Promise realizes that the Angel's lips are not moving. She is speaking directly into her mind.

"Ah ha! A telepath. I love it. How'd you get up here? she asks.

"Actually I fell down here from up there. From Heaven," The Angel replies, very matter-of-factly.

"Now wait a second. Are you here for me? Because I am not ready to die. I am just getting started," Promise says nervously.

"I am not here for you," The Angel says.

Promise exhales with relief.

"You sure are a big girl. At least seven feet I'd say," Promise says, standing to touch the Angel's dress.

"Wow, this fabric is amazing. I've never seen anything like this on Earth. Oh dear God! You're not breathing!"

"It just looks that way. I am breathing, on the inside," she says.

"What happened to you?" Promise asks

"I was heading back home and suddenly I was confused and didn't know where I was anymore. Next thing I remember is falling and falling and then I am here inside of a body and heavy as stone, I can't move at all," The Angel explains.

Promise tries to grasp the Angel's condition and what might be the reason for it.

"You know, this sounds very similar to what the Bees have been going through. Colony collapse disorder. The Bees get confused and disoriented and can't remember where their hives are. They eventually get lost and die," Promise regrets saying that last bit.

"Angels do not die," The Angel assures her.

This talk of Bees reminds Promise, she must return to New Witch to tend her hives this afternoon.

"I hate leaving you here all alone, but I've got to get back home. My Bees are swarming today. How do we stay in touch? What's your name?

"I am who you to choose to see," The Angel says again.

"So, I get to choose what to call you? OK. How about the name of my favorite stone? Onyx."

Onyx's eyes twinkle at the sound of her name.

"Onyx will be here when you return," Onyx replies.

"Oh, I do hope so," Promise says, placing her hands over her heart.

"Onyx, I shall return," she says, bowing to Onyx.

Promise turns to fetch the besom broom she left leaning near the stairwell door since morning. It's handle is a globe of Citrine and its broom grass a brilliant shade of Tangerine.

Straddling it like a horse, Promise leaps into the air, with her legs kicking about wildly.

Waving to Onyx, she begins singing full throttle in her raspy contralto voice.

"*Mama gave me, Mama gave me, Mama gave me,*
My very own Angel"

Onyx rolls her eyes.

13

Grandmother Promise Bee Keeper Supreme

Grandmother Promise returns to New Witch still buzzing from her encounter with Onyx.

"New Witch Honey is out of this world," Promise says laughing to herself, as she imagines placing honey on Onyx's lips.

Drawing honey from the hive is Promise's favorite task. Bee drone is music to her ears. Honey shimmering in the sunlight.

Promise remembers that Onyx might be listening in and continues as if having a conversation with her.

"Our Honey ranges from a palest of violet to a deep crimson. Adding layers of crushed gemstones was my brilliant idea. Edible by ways of a Witchery only known to us. Some magics are best left hidden, so as not to expose them to contamination by any greedy profiteers below. Glorious tells his customers the gems are crystallized honey, make believe gems, just for a Faery touch. He comes up with wonderful alibis and decoys in lickety-split time. Just like his old Grandma." Promise cackles to herself.

"Oh goody, here comes the swarm. Hello Girls."

14

An Angel Lands In New Witch Forest

An Angel has fallen into the highest branches of Mother Oak. A monstrous beauty with long pale blue hair, translucent skin and opalescent wings. It is hanging upside down, swinging back and forth with its arms swaying in slow motion and making strange bird like sounds in a very high pitched voice.

"This feels sooooo good," the Angel says.

Unlike the Angels who fall to Earth, by landing in New Witch this Angel has fallen between the worlds. Here it is both ethereal and physical, fully animated and quite physically human.

Dangling above from the same tree Euphoria is hidden under, the Angel's squealing delight has caused the mound of moss beneath Mother Oak to start separating, pushing up a very much disturbed Euphoria Green from her womb like retreat. With flecks of mica all over her skin, violets and bluebells strewn in her hair, she stands up shaking them off like a wolf in the rain.

Euphoria takes a few steps back to see what all the racket is about. Lo and Behold, it is another Angel.

"What next?" Euphoria says, exasperated.

"This feels soooooooo good." The Angel says, drawing her words out taffy.

Euphoria starts to laugh.

"You look like an upside down Christmas ornament," she teases.

"Up-side down Christmas is soooo good," The Angel replies.

"Whenever you are ready, let me know, I'll help you get down," Euphoria offers.

"Ready now," The Angel responds.

Euphoria rises into the air, positions herself and instructs,

"Now reach behind you and put your arms around my waist. I am going to lift your legs off the branch and drop them over my shoulders."

The Angel takes forever, but finally gets it's arms around Euphoria's waist. Euphoria carefully untangles her legs and sets them over her shoulders.

"Hold on tight," she says, floating gently down to the ground. The Angel releases her arms from Euphoria's waist and does a backward flip in slow motion. Face to face, there is that same deep sense of recognition between them, only this time the energy is one of pure joy.

"I am who you choose to see," The Angel says.

Euphoria's eyes darken,

"I've heard that one before," she says sadly.

"Desire is the calling force of the Universe, the maker of all things. Desire creates and Desire destroys," The Angel says.

Euphoria, surprised by the Angels response, considers carefully what she should call her.

"Your eyes remind me of emeralds. What about Emeraldine?"

"Em.er.al.dine," the Angel repeats and squeals with delight, clasping her hands together, she starts bouncing up and down just like an astronaut on the moon.

"How do you Emeraldine. I am Euphoria Green," Euphoria says, shaking her hand.

Deciding that Emeraldine probably needs to eat something to help her body adjust to the gravity of New Witch, she asks,

"Are you hungry?"

"Yes Euphoria Green, I am, I am. Hungry," Emeraldine squeals.

"Then let us go to my house. This way." Euphoria says.

Taking Emeraldine by the hand Euphoria begins skipping from sheer excitement, which sets Emeraldine bouncing in the air after her like a big pale blue balloon.

"You are going to love Grandmother Promise and my darling brother Glorious and our precious cat Prunella and our Dryad Witch Hazel. We all live together inside our Casa Bella. Casa is Italian for house and Bella means beautiful, but sometimes, she's a monster, so watch out!"

When they arrive, Bella the House, who has ears all over New Witch, has already prepared the table. There are two crystal goblets and two crystal soup bowls and a huge crystal platter in the center of the table, two silver spoons, two silver forks, two silver butter knives and two linen napkins.

"Bella, I see you've been eaves dropping again," Euphoria says.

Bella blushes and the kitchen walls turn the color pink.

"It's OK Bella. Thank you for setting the table," Euphoria strokes the wall and Bella sighs, the walls quickly change back to white again.

"What a house! So alive. So sensitive. This is a special place," Emeraldine begins to sing.

SONG
BETWEEN HEAVEN AND EARTH

Between Heaven and Earth
Between Sunlight and Starlight
The World is a Circle
A Spiral of Kindness

Between Daylight and Darkness
Between Winter and Summer
The Seasons Delight Us
They Teach Us to Wonder

How many times did I want to take root
How many times did I wish I could stay
Dreaming of Magic and what it must be like
To be here on the ground
Gravity holding me down

Between Heaven and Earth
Between Morning and Night
Between Living and Dying
And all that can Happen
A Universe A Lifetime Eternity Inside Us
Between Heaven and Earth

15

Euphoria and Emeraldine Feast

"You'll be more comfortable on this" Euphoria says, placing a stool at the table on behalf of Emeraldines wings. She pours sparkling water from their well into the two crystal goblets and then raises her glass high. Emeraldine mimics her.
"To new beginnings," Euphoria says in a toast to Emeraldine.
　Both are simply beaming at one another and Euphoria thinks, 'We shall become the best of friends.'
"The very best of friends," Emeraldine says.
　Can Emeraldine can hear her thoughts?" Euphoria wonders, blushing at the thought.
　In minutes Euphoria has thrown together a sumptuous feast. Pumpkin soup is soon steaming in a large copper pot, while outside in the Enchantment Garden she gathers fresh arugula, cherry tomatoes, red bell pepper, cucumbers, celery and dill for their salad. Then she cuts generous slices of homemade sprouted bread and serves it with tiny bowls of whipped herb butter.

"There's Cherry Tarts for dessert. Normally we'd have our dessert first, but something tells me afterwards will be is better."

Emeraldine is rocking sideways on her stool and humming "Ummmm," then lowering her head she sniffs her soup, sniffs her salad and sniffs the bread, just like a cat.

"Do you always sleep under a tree?" she pauses to ask, several mouthfuls later.

"Oh no, that was a special circumstance." Euphoria answers quickly then changes the subject.

"But good thing I did, or you'd still be dangling upside down," she adds and they both start to laugh.

"I have an excellent bed upstairs and the softest downy quilts and pillows. As my guest, you will as well." Euphoria adds.

"Normally I would have been on my Sigil flight over Manhattan Isle. Best time for weaving blessings is the before dawn. We all curse and bless, hex and pray, invoke and provoke, unconsciously swinging on the pendulum of duality. My Sigil flight is to infuse the city with more the light. My prayer is that Manhattan Isle be restored to God's original plan."

Emeraldine's face suddenly changes expression.

"God knows himself through his Creation. The human species called us into being once they became aware of God. The same way an infant becomes aware of its mother and father. It calls out to them with its voice, with its heart, for what it needs and desires. Human desires and human needs called out to us, created us to aid them, to comfort them, to guide them, to protect them, to rescue them, to give them hope and faith in their own abilities. That's right, they created Us. Our falling to Earth is also their creation."

"I don't understand, " Euphoria says, confused.

"You were created by them as well," Emeraldine admits.

"Are you saying I don't really exist?" Euphoria's eyes widen.

"You most certainly do exist. But you have been created by their need and desire to have ones such as you."

"What about my own needs and desires? I've known them since moment I was strapped on to Grandmother Promise's back and saw the skyline of Manhattan Isle. Waves of ecstatic knowing rushed into my tiny heart. I could feel the raw power of the island's soul. I knew then, this island was mine to protect," Euphoria finishes, apparently ruffled at having to defend her existence.

"Tell me more," Emeraldine requests.

Euphoria exhales and settles down. Actually she is thrilled to finally have someone to talk honestly about her family with.

"My family's legacy is rooted in the bedrock of Manhattan Isle. We are descendants of the native people of Manhatta, the Lenape. This was their homeland until the Dutch arrived and built New Amsterdam. By 1642, war between the Dutch and English settlers threatened the Lenape from both sides.

Our great-great-great Lenape Grandmother prayed for guidance and was told in her dream where she should take her family to escape being slaughtered. Her name was Kahesena Haki, Lenape for Our Mother Earth. Her vision revealed a cave at the island's most northern tip. She saw her family going into the cave, through a long tunnel and then climbing up a ladder to safety.

Following her vision she led her family, great-great great Grandfather Onkuntewakan, whose name means Blessing From Heaven, their son and daughter and two Dutch orphans, a brother and sister, through the cave's tunnel to its very end and found the ladder. The ladder was several miles long. They climbed it for three days. They could see layers of ancient earth as they climbed, then layers of azure sky by day and layers of dazzling starlight millions of years old, by night.

By the end of the third day, they had climbed right into our forest. They were magically ' witched up,' miraculously saved by unseen forces. And here we are, four hundred years later and still invisible to those living on Manhattan Isle."

Euphoria's Circle of Stars have been spinning during her tale. Emeraldine, mesmerized by them, begins laughing.

"Look at your eyes."

"From the moment I emerged from my mother's womb, I had tiny stars rotating in my eyes. Mother named me Euphoria for that reason. It happens whenever I feel intense pleasure. I've always known the power of pleasure and its absence causes me great discomfort and angst. Whereas my brother Glorious, rises to his name regardless of what life throws at him. He'll turn disappointment or any obstacle into victory and enjoy the entire process no matter what the odds," Euphoria boasts happily.

Emeraldine who has been listening with rapt attention, has also managed to polish off two bowls of Pumpkin soup, an extra heaping of salad, three slices of sprouted bread drenched in butter, along with several cups of mint tea. Her body swelled so that she can barely fit on her stool. Her wings are now fully extended.

"Emeraldine, you look like you can fly again. Eat and run, is that your plan? " Euphoria teases her.

"Let's see," Emeraldine says excited.

Popping off of her stool she maneuvers her self sideways to get through the kitchen door. Outside she tries using her wings. But like an open umbrella, they have no lifting power whatsoever.

"I guess my wings were hungry too. Look at how big they are," she says sadly.

Closing her eyes, Emeraldine goes silent and stands very still.

Euphoria leaves her in the Enchantment Garden.

They both need to rest.

16

Angels On the News

News regarding the falling Angels was initially explained as a spectacular Flash Mob event. Trying to justify it as a theatrical promotional gimmick. But by whom? No one seems to know.

As days pass with more and more Angel sightings being reported world wide, it is apparent this is not a theatrical event.

Angels are dropping like flies out of no where on anyone's radar. They are landing on the ground, on top of buildings, in the middle of roads, in lakes and rivers. There they remain fixed like stone. The fact their eyes are alive and visibly responsive is beyond any one's comprehension. Conscious yet inert, staggeringly beautiful to behold. Apparently indestructible, as military attempts to removing them has failed over and over again.

Governments are now accusing one another for a situation that has gotten entirely out of control. Traffic diverted, supply chains and transportation re routed. All normal activity ceases, as citizens world wide focus upon the Angels. If it is not an invasion. If it is not a natural disaster. Then what is it?

17

Jade Cortez & Pearl Hill

Jade Cortez and Pearl Hill have been partners for eleven years. They live and work together in what was once a warehouse owned by Pearl's Great Grandfather, near Chinatown.

Jade is an artist. Everything she does she makes more beautiful. The Black Needle, occupies one half of the ground floor of the warehouse and is regarded as a sacred space in their community. A place where one steps into a vortex of meaningful intent, where the human body is both canvas and cauldron. Her clients are encouraged to explore the purpose behind their desired design. The tattoo itself becomes a catalyst for self discovery and illumination.

Jade loves the process of making her own ink. Using only the purest plants and minerals to make irresistible hues of red umber, burnt orange, copper, pecan, chocolate, ochre, slate, moss, fern, evergreen and lime. Also adding indigo to expand her earth tone palette into shades of violet, fuchsia, mulberry, lavender, aquamarine, teal, turquoise and midnight blue.

Jade was born in Ecuador. Her mother, Esmeralda Cortez is one of seven generations of *Curandera*, medicine women. Jade's father, a farmer, was killed when Jade was six years old. She and her four siblings and mother immigrated to America twenty years ago.

Although not formally trained as a *Curandera*, Jade carries her mother's wisdom in her bones. It lives in her intuitive perception of the world. Spirits are everywhere. Positive ones and negative ones. The latter being those may attach to us, by way of invisible cords and bind us, if we are not consciously aligned with the light. Knowing this, Jades prays over her tattoos, so that they become amulets of protection, potent, discreet and fortifying.

Pearl Hill's acupuncture clinic occupies the other half of The Black Needle. Pearl inherited her passion for healing from her great grandfather, Chase Hill.

Doctor Hill traveled to China in the 1930s to study Classical Chinese medicine. When he returned to America he made his fortune selling medicinal herbs in Chinatown. Pearl has named the clinic treatment rooms in his honor, using his favorite medicinals, Clove, Thyme, Ginger and Cinnamon.

Pearl sees every human being as a glorious, miraculous unfolding of consciousness. Albeit riddled with contradiction, at war within ourselves, geniuses at camouflage, ultimately tripping ourselves up and giving ourselves away, we are all worthy of unconditional love.

That is what Pearl Hill consistently offers and generously gives. The Black Needle Acupuncture clinic is a healing oasis for people in need of affordable, natural medicine. Even the vibe Pearl has created, playing smooth operator Sade and jazz goddesses like Betty Carter, Abbey Lincoln and Nina Simone, is top notch. No sleepy new age tuneless tunes going down at The Black Needle. Clients love her soul sensibility and her needle working mojo. A true healer in every sense of the word, Pearl listens with her whole heart and her clients know it.

Pearl has been attending Euphoria Green's Herbal Wisdom class every Sunday morning at Faery Cakes. She is first to testify that Euphoria's herbal apothecary is most outstanding in purity and potency. She purchases all her medicinal herbs and spices directly from her.

Jade and Pearl are in their loft upstairs unpacking groceries.

"I swear Euphoria reads my mind every time I place an order. Even before I tell her what I need, she'll tell me she's just picked that exact item fresh from her garden." Pearl says, while opening a new batch of Super Bee Pollen.

"Well, what do you expect? " Jade says grinning. "She be witch!"

"Pot calling the kettle black? " Pearl adds. They both laugh.

"Now just look at this Bee Pollen. Have you ever seen Bee Pollen like this before? They are almost the size of corn kernels. And there's a recipe too," Pearl says, showing Jade the little handwritten note from Euphoria.

Bee Pollen Beauty Drink
In a food processor add:
1 Peeled Orange
1/2 freshly squeezed Lemon
1 Tbsp. Collagen Powder
1 Tbsp. Bee Pollen,
1 Tbsp. Honey
7 fl Oz of Raw Milk
Mix well
Can also be used as a facial mask.

18

Promise Returns To Onyx

"I couldn't sleep thinking about you being stuck here all alone," Promise confesses.

"Never alone," Onyx replies.

"Can you communicate with the other Angels?" Promise asks, removing her cloak and spreading it out on the roof to sit on.

"Yes."

Onyx begins humming. The sound is so powerful, it feels like the entire galaxy is vibrating inside Promise's body. Curling into a fetal position she begins weeping uncontrollably. Onyx pauses.

"Too strong for you," Onyx says.

Promise rolls over on to her back and exclaims, "Now that was incredible. I feel so much better. I really needed to cry. It has been so long since I let myself just go like that. I live with my grandchildren and I rarely let them see me fall apart," Promise confesses while blowing her nose. "There's so much inside of me that I never share with them."

"You can share it with me. I'm not going anywhere," Onyx says.

"True. You are my captive audience," Promise says grinning wildly, she moves in closer nearer to Onyx's feet. "Oh, but where to begin?" Promise says holding her knees, rocking back and forth while preparing to tell Onyx her story.

"It all started over a century ago. I was researching Opulence as my subject in personal evolution. I needed to see it for myself. All the places I had heard about. The vast kingdoms and palaces, the castles, the temples. To observe them first hand and meet those whose wealth and power has ruled the world for countless ages. So I set out to travel across the seas. I saw luxuries too magnificent to comprehend. I held my tongue and feigned only the most non plus, understated reaction to all that I saw. All the while these marvels unraveled deep activity within my bone marrow. My blood changed, my corpuscles rearranged themselves into new codes. The language of my desire split into a myriad of dialects. I was obsessed with seeking the best of the best. One must be exposed to the possibility of it, before one can image it. The gradations of refinement were infinite. But then to my astonishment, my research morphed into creation.

I became the Opulence I witnessed. Without arrogance, without conceit, I rose in stature. I became famous overnight. Famous for what, you may ask? I have no idea! Books have been written about me. Films made about my life. Dances choreographed in my honor. Theaters, libraries, streets, all named after me. I am so adored, that the collective thought form of me orbits the Earth like an additional moon.

What is it like to be me, you may ask? That my child is for you to discover. Go forth into the world on your own two feet. Be brave, be cunning, be curious. See what you see. Let it work upon your blood. And viola! You'll understand who I am."

Onyx has been listening intently with her eyes closed,
"If only I could take one single step, I would," she thinks.

19

Onyx Is Thinking

Next morning Onyx is thinking.
"I could get used to this. Being substantial, having a body even if I can't move it. It lets me taste being somewhere instead of everywhere. I like being on this rooftop. I can see day breaking and stars coming out at night. Best of all, I love reading Promise's mind. Her mind overflows with faces and places and recipes and music."

Onyx's eyes are glowing with pleasure.

"What a lucky Angel am I to have landed here. I can hear the traffic below and people's voices. I can hear someone playing the piano across the street right now. How wonderful it is to have physical ears. To hear sounds from only one location. That must be it. Limitation can be soothing. Ah, this is so sweet."

Onyx starts to hum the melody being played on the piano. Her humming frightens nearby birds and sends them fluttering away.

"Oh dear, I must remember to hold back."

Eyes closed, Onyx withdraws into her essence of infinite light.

20

Euphoria & Emeraldine Next Morning

The morning is bright with stars and everything is out of place and inside out. Sweaters, socks, sheets, towels off the shelves, out of their drawers. Doors that had been locked are open. Clock hands wound backwards. Thank God for the aroma of coffee brewing. That still works right.

Euphoria goes downstairs into the kitchen and finds Emeraldine bouncing about like an astronaut on the moon. Emeraldine is mixing pancake batter in a bowl. When she sees Euphoria she stops and offers her a cup of fresh brewed coffee.

"Guten Morgen," Emeraldine coos.

"Sprechen de Deutsch?" Euphoria counters.

"Un Bissel, " Emeraldine replies.

Euphoria grins, "That's Yiddish."

Emeraldine shouts, "Allah Akbar."

Euphoria takes a sip of her coffee.

"This is delicious. What's in it?"

Emeraldine opens her palm revealing two blue pearl flowers.

Euphoria is surprised,

"Moon babies? But I only planted them yesterday."

"I used one of your Quicken Spells this morning to move things along a little faster," Emeraldine confesses.

Now Euphoria is ruffled.

"Emeraldine, just because you can read my mind does not mean you can use my spells without asking my permission. AND going through all my closets like you're exploring a cave is not acceptable either!"

Emeraldine's face goes flat.

"I'm still confused about what is and what is not, acceptable. Angels read human minds, it is natural to us. But I see being in a body changes things. There are rules for having bodies and even more rules for being with Witchess. I apologize. Please do not give up on me. I am a quick learner."

Emeraldine points to a plate stacked with pancakes,

"Look, I've just made you your favorite buckwheat pancakes with black sesame seeds and crushed pistachios, topped with Kiwi sauce infused with mint, lime juice, honey and Matcha tea. Did you know Matcha tea contains a caffeine that is different from coffee. It slowly releases energy over the course of several hours to help restore hormonal balance and is beneficial to the adrenal glands," Emeraldine rattles off in a single breath.

"You are a quick learner," Euphoria says, trying not to smile.

"Okay, we'll figure it out as we go along." Euphoria says, going into the pantry to get a sparkling red jar.

"Check this out," putting a spoonful into Emeraldine's mouth.

Emeraldine shudders, lets out an orgasmic moan and spins like a top. When she finally recovers, she says breathlessly,

"Oooooh, I must eat my pancakes with this honey lying down or else I shall spin into a crystal ball and roll away."

21

Euphoria Tells About Bella The House

"I'll ask Bella to open up the breakfast room. There's a fainting couch in there you can use," Euphoria offers laughing.

Emeraldine's eyes widen.

"Where does Bella's magic come from?"

Euphoria shrugs,

"We're not exactly sure. Everyday we wake up to a slightly different house. Our bedrooms, bathrooms and the kitchen are off limits to Bella's magic. Other wise we'd never get a good nights rest or prepare our meals on time. Other than those rooms, we never know what we'll find down the hall or behind a new door.

Bella The House came with her name and a heart so big it reaches Riverside Drive, down below. Like a tree growing upside down, her energy branches out like a curtain over Grants Tomb. That is how we Witchess travel back and forth so easily.

"When you speak she understands you," Emeraldine points out.

"Yes, she understands everything we say and she knows what we are thinking before we say a word. She answers us using things in the house. The walls will change color, the windows will open or shut, objects will move around," Euphoria adds.

Then she strikes a dramatic pose.

"Imagine rooms that expand, and rooms that contract. Imagine rooms that breathe in, and rooms that breathe out. Imagine doors that groan and doors purr. Depending who is inside or whom she prefers."

Motioning for Emeraldine to come closer, she lowers her voice so Bella will not hear her.

"Bella dances in rain and sways like a hula girl. We find puddles in the cupboards where the dishes have been bathed in rainwater." Emeraldine covers her mouth to stop giggling.

"Bella was built by our great, great, great Grandparents. Once while I was cleaning out one of her many closets, she slid a wooden box out of a tiny hidden door in the wall. It was filled with the tools our ancestors used to build Bella. Not your typical kind of tools made from metal and wood, but tools made of crystal and nails made of silver and gold. There were strange cords and stones in a leather pouch. And a quill pen and clay jar with ink still fresh inside. After I had seen everything in the box, Bella pulled it back again through the tiny door and then the door disappeared."

Euphoria pauses to let Emeraldine take in the mystery of it all.

"Even though she cleans up after herself easily enough, Bella adores being cleaned by us. We do it with the utmost care and attention. Every stone and shingle, every board and nail. We oil the wood and polish the silver and brass with joy. When we're done Bella sparkles and sighs in contentment. She loves it when we bake and brew and when we poach and stew. The fragrances please her. In a strange way we are her garden. She loves the scent of us, the full intent of us, the unpredictable invention of us."

"The one thing she is very shy about is singing in front of us. She stops as soon as she hears us approaching. So sometimes we'll hover a while in the mists and clouds just to hear her sing. As soon as Bella believes we too far away to hear her, she starts singing in French, then she complains in Italian, brags about her rooms in German, flaunts her interior design style in Swedish, as if she is on stage in front of an audience. Recently I've heard her sing something that sounds like it's from a Broadway musical."

Emeraldine winks at Euphoria and telepathically suggests,

"Ask me if I'd like to go gather mushrooms deep in the forest."

Euphoria's eyes light up and nods her head YES.

"Emeraldine, how would you like to go gather some delicious mushrooms in the forest?" Euphoria says.

"Why yes, of course. I love mushrooms. Let's go right now." Emeraldine replies.

22

Bella the House

Bella has heard every word Euphoria has told Emeraldine. She plays along and sings "En Vie Rose" full throttle. Then making a dramatic exit she unravels a red carpet down a long hallway ending in gold gilded doors that open to the most magnificent miniature theater. A spot light hits center stage and Bella's voice comes cascading through the rafters singing a song from her musical.

<u>BELLA MAGIQUE</u>
Rooms appear as occasion needs
Halls and stairs, theaters and balconies
Ballrooms and lagoons, hot pools and nurseries
All hidden deep inside of me

I Am Bella Magique
Maison Du être, Magnifique
Look at my Windows. Look at my Floors.
Have you ever seen anything as magical before?

I Am Bella Magique
Maison Du être, Magnifique
Look at my Ceilings. Look at my Doors.
Have you ever seen anything this magical before?

Bella Recites:
Can you imagine having a house such as I?
I can create as many rooms as you desire
And when you're ready to leave them at night,
I make them disappear, completely out of sight
No need to polish, nor vacuum, nor wash, nor dust
Not only am I economical.
I'm totally secure and entirely phenomenal

I Am Bella Magique
Maison Du être, Magnifique
Look at my Ceilings. Look at my Doors.
Have you ever seen anything this magical before?

While my Witchess are busy harvesting and brewing
Potions and lotions, baking and stewing
I am here to assist, never do I tire
I lend them extra hands and extra feet
As the need arises
Less is More, if you request.
Spacious or Cozy, Opulent or Modest
Rooms that Breathe, Doors that Enchant
Dishes and kettles, Pots and pans
Beds that float, Floors that dance
Whatever it is, Just ASK!

Prunella the Cat has just wandered into the theater and makes her way down the center aisle to sit front row. Inspired by Prunella's presence in the audience, Bella launches into an impromptu cat themed monologue just for her.

" If a house is a Cat, And what house is a Cat?
Well, that's exactly that, Bella is!
With every morsel of her mortar, She stretches every dawn,
A little bit to the left and a little bit to the right,
One wall goes west and one wall goes east,
Until every room has twisted its corners and its seams.
Cupola's go a swaying and weather vanes twirl,
Chimneys go bobbing, bricks inhale, pipes unfurl.
A generous spine and paws that scratch.
Yes, tis' true, tis' true, Bella is a house that is just like a Cat."

Bella repeats the last line over and over until it ends in a whisper. Then she gets very quiet and thoughtful.
"It must be intermission," Prunella says to herself.
"I wonder what it feels like to be on stage?"
Prunella leaps into the spotlight, inhales and places both front paws together at her waist, in her best Cat Contralto she sings.
"While Bella sleeps She dreams of rooms,
She's seen in book from in our Library,
From every age and continent,
In endless hues of silk, wool and velvet."
Bella doe not stir. Clearly her mind is elsewhere.
Prunella continues en soto voce,
"It is just like baking a cake. I use the finest ingredients I can get. I measure them exactmont. *I always mix with Love* " She sings,

Her voice finally jolts Bella out of her reverie. Responding as if on cue, Bella sings,

Love can bake a cake, Love can build a house,
Love can grow a garden, Love can warm a mouse....

Prunella interrupts,

"Warm a mouse?"

"Yes my dear. Not all mice should be made into muffins. Mushrooms are a wonderful substitute for mouse. Come, let me show you the best ones. I've hidden them especially for you and you alone my precious," Bella coos.

Then she lures Prunella outside by waving a conductor's baton in the air.

Prunella seriously doubts that mushrooms are a good substitute for mouse, but she indulges Bella and follows her baton out into the Enchantment Garden, just in case they are.

23

Prunella The Cat

Prunella The Cat has the softest lavender fur and huge gold but sometimes violet eyes. She is so silky and fluffy to the touch and has long ballerina legs and huge nimble paws. Paws that can flip pancakes, pour honey and slice and dice and stir purrrfectly!

"A Day Of Pancakes," Prunella announces to no one.

Whisking three Green Blue Eggs, she then adds 1/4 cup of Topaz Gemstone Honey, two tablespoons of Coconut Oil and 1/2 cup Fresh Cream.

"Even a cat can make pancakes!" Prunella thinks out loud most all the time, even when no one is there to hear her.

"A huge Bengal tiger chased me in my dream last. I wonder what it means? Could it represent fear of sexual intimacy? Or perhaps fear of my tigress powers? Could it be a warning of some impending danger?" she asks, pouring the batter into the frying pan.

Prunella asks, then decides she does not need to decide.

"A Witchess cat does not need to have the answer. All that we require are interesting questions. The art of asking the right questions is what I, Prunella the Cat excel at."

Born and raised in New Witch, Prunella has been completely ensconced in a wonderland of opportunities and options.

She can cook her meals or catch them in the wild, but prefers the later. She is often found labeling jars of her own spices to add special touches to her recipes.

The Greens have encouraged Prunella's passion for cooking by building her, her very own kitchen inside of theirs, including a purrfectly cat sized stove, sink, counter, cupboard and refrigerator.

Oh how Prunella loves to bake. Her specialties are Cat Nippy Rolls and Mousey Muffins. She also poaches Ducky Egg Pies and brews her favorite, Snaily Broth Soup.

Most of her creations are welcome by Bella, but occasionally some are gently removed and either placed outside the door or quickly flung out the window before anyone else sees or smells them.

Since Prunella was a wee kitten, Euphoria has been teaching her food charms. Charms she believes confirm she was destined to be a cook.

"Flavor, flavor, sample, savor,
Take one bite, you're mine forever."

"It's more than a house and I'm more than a mouse, " Prunella declares as she lifts her tray of freshly baked Mousey Muffins and proceeds out doors into the Enchantment Garden for her daily Cat Nip tea and savory treats with Witch Hazel the Dryad who joins her to sip and gobble away.

"These mice taste just like mushrooms, so I can't understand why Promise and Euphoria turn their noses up whenever I offer them a muffin," Prunella says with her lips pinching up into a cat pout.

"Well, I suppose it's the image of a dead mouse that turns their stomachs. After all, mice are God's creatures too. They too have value and a purpose on Earth. And I personally adore them," Witch Hazel adds.

Prunella turns her head away from Witch Hazel, clearly now in a bad mood feeling guilty.

"Well, I am a cat and that's what we cats do. We eat mice. I know for a fact that on Manhattan Isle people adore us for eating their mice. At least that's what I've heard," she retorts.

"I doubt that any of those cats have their own kitchen or even know how to bake," Witch Hazel reminds her.

Prunella perks up to Witch Hazel's brighter note.

"I simply can't imagine what life would be like without having my own kitchen. Not being able to bake and brew, poach and stew, fry and steam, puree and cream, stir and toss, blend and pour? What kind of life would that be? I'd be so bored," Prunella realizes.

"There you see. You have the best of both worlds right here. And besides, if everyone loved your Mousey Muffins, you'd end up spending all your time baking them for Faery Cakes and have no time left to do anything else," Witch Hazel points out.

"Witch Hazel, you are a genius. I can't thank you enough for pointing this out to me. From now on no more complaints from me. I am one true cat contentment."

Prunella hugs herself, then hugs Witch Hazel and runs back into her kitchen to give thanks and praise.

"Dear God, Thank you, thank you for making sure no one likes my Mousey Muffins or my Cat Nippy Rolls or my Snaily Broth or my Ducky Egg Pies or my Lizard Tarts or my Froggy Custard Cake or my Butterfly Salad or my Fire Fly Ice Cream."

24

Angel Helios

He came through the World Trade Center Station with only a slight warp to a ceiling's glass panel. Thankfully no one was there to witness his arrival at 4:00 am on Sunday morning.

Over nine feet tall, iridescent wings, wavy alabaster hair and pale pearl like iridescent eyes. A radiant crown upon his head emitting a strange glow, with spokes not unlike Lady Liberty's.

Around 8:00 am Pearl Hill is on her way uptown to Euphoria's herbal wisdom class. She had planned to head up there early, get out at 96th Street and walk the rest of the way through Riverside Park before heading over to Faery Cakes.

There are very few people in the station's central lobby when she arrives. They are all, as she is about to be, transfixed on the spot. Watching the Angel's translucent skin morphing into a mirror like surface. In a few moments everyone there is able to see their own faces reflecting back to them when looking at his body.

Pearl hears someone speaking to her.

"I am who you choose to see," a beautiful baritone voice says.

Pearl's first thought was that this must be some kind of flash mob theater performance. Deciding to play along she thinks of the Greek Sun God, Helios.

"Helios is good," the Angel says.

Pearl is confused.

"How did he do that?"

She looks around and observes other people are having similar expressions of shock and surprise on their faces.

Aware she will be late for class, Pearl tears herself away and makes it down to the subway platform just as her train approaches.

Her mind begins streaming poetic, as it often does while riding the harsh metal cars. Still buzzing from communion with Helios, she directs her thoughts to him.

"Beauty in the dust. Beauty in the rust. Beauty in the mold. Beauty in the fungus. Everything deserves respect. The stench of this subway amid the racket of this city's unnatural assembly, where every square inch is crammed with concrete and engulfed in wireless skin. Not the Manhattan I knew as a child. Every day my heart stretches wider and wider to embrace it all and give it more love. I too, walk her streets towards my destinations, ride the rhythms of her madness," she tells him.

The train comes to a screeching halt at 96th Street station. Pearl gets out and walks west, inhaling the warm breeze of the river.

"Manhattan is a hive. People are swarming here as well. Another colony collapse going on right here. Just like our Bees, only this is one is staged to look like something else. A theater built by slaves for slaves. No one is free here," she concludes.

En route to her class, Pearl soaks up the heavenly fragrances of red and pink cherry blossoms, in full splendor this May morning.

25

Euphoria's Herbal Wisdom Class

When Pearl joins Euphoria's class, all of the women are talking loud and excited about Manhattan Isle's Angel sightings. Euphoria is seated with her eyes closed, waiting for them to settle down. Finally they do.

"Now ladies, let's gather all that energy and focus it back into our bodies. Close your eyes, sit up straight, lengthen your spine, lift your pelvic floor and breathe deeply into your lower back," Euphoria's mellifluous voice embraces the room.

This morning she begins the class by reading aloud from Witch Hazel's book, entitled The Daughters Of Terra Flora.

"*The Daughters of Terra Flora were given the secret notes to each flower. Each note could only be heard by the Daughter within her own mind. It was not a shared note. It was not a sung note. It was a note that came and went upon each listening by the Daughter herself. The Daughter is genuine. She knows flowers speak with sacred intimacy. That such intimacy is a delicate, fragile thing. It can be broken by harsh thoughts. So the Daughter learns to soothe her own mind, before she gathers any flowers. So, we begin at the beginning. When the beginning is good, all will proceed well,"* Euphoria pauses.

"So my greedy ones, you came here today to gather nectar from my mind like little hungry bees, but first, we are going to examine your minds. Herbal Wisdom is not just about knowing the names and properties of each plant. It is about cultivating a special receptivity within your consciousness. To receive the intelligence each plant offers is not a one way street. It's not, plants give and you take. It is a relationship between partners with a long courtship.

A sensitive, sensual awareness that is of mutual consent or else it is rape! There are penalties for rape in the plant kingdom. Our entire planet is suffering from our passive consent to the rape of all our plants and animals.

Just as our Bees are being afflicted by colony collapse disorder, Heaven is also losing its hive. Why are Angels falling among us now? Why do you think they are here? Why are they paralyzed? They can no longer help us. They no longer can save us. We are on our own now, more than ever before. Nature is offering us a window of opportunity, a path of right action. We can help ourselves. We can save ourselves," Euphoria says.

The class ripples with consent. They are in total accord with Euphoria's predilections.

"This may be the most important work you'll ever do. That is why you are here. A real medicine woman keeps her magic to herself. She does not brag about her craft. She does not boast about her powers. She knows less is more, especially when dealing with others. Fewer words, fewer tools, fewer rituals.

She listens within to her own inner Elementals. Her bones are the earth, her blood is the water, her breath is the air, her desire is the fire. She knows her body is a cauldron. Even as she sleeps, the brew simmers. So potent is her inner elixir, its effects trail behind her like a bridal veil. So volatile is her inner potion, the air parts wherever she walks.

She is a tree amongst trees, a flower amongst flowers, a stone amongst stones, a raindrop in the rain, a moonbeam in the moonlight. She sings, she shines, she blossoms, she bears fruit, she nourishes and sustains. She is the tone within every chord. All living on Earth vibrate its strings, beat upon its skin, blow upon its horns, rattle it, shake it, bow it, stroke it. There is no silence anywhere. All is symphony. No breaks, no pauses, no rests. One continuous flow, one infinite, eternal music."

Euphoria has been dramatically punctuating her words with extended arms and hand gestures. Finally they come to rest at her side. All the women take a deep breath and sigh in unison.

"Let us ponder this vision together now. See yourself in your own mind approaching a landscape you know. What is there? Plants? No! They are not Plants. They are living beings, just as you are. Every leaf, bud, blossom, branch, fruit and flower is a living being.

Think of how you approach one another in this class, when you come through the door. How you acknowledge and show mutual respect to one another, how you greet each other. How you take the time to sense each other's energy. Can you give that awareness, that kindness and respect to each plant, in your minds eye. Can you see them truly, truly see them?"

Several women begin weeping. A profound wave of humility sweeps through the room. The curtains on the cafe windows begin to flutter. Suddenly everyone feels a tingling sensation, running up and down their arms and spine.

"Ah ha. I believe we have guests come to join us. Let us give welcome to the Flower Devas. It is they who have heard our call and are here to witness our awakening."

26

The Enchantment Garden

New Witch, New York receives the rays of the sun and light of the moon as if it were still the year of 1642. The skies are clear as crystal, the soil loamy rich and sweet with micro organisms. The passage of time swirls around New Witch, but cannot alter her original frequency codes. The river running to the streams running to the lake carry abundant fish, shimmering beneath sparkling emerald waters

Those living below on Manhattan Isle now cannot even begin to imagine how water should really taste. Fortunate are those who make their way uptown to eat at Faery Cakes where salads glisten like jewels and life's original force oozes in every dish served. Customers claim they are bewitched just by looking into their bowls.

Planting season starts in Aprilarium. Euphoria uses seeds she has saved from last years harvest for this year's crop. In New Witch seeds plant themselves. That is because they know exactly where they want to go. All Euphoria has to do is hold the seeds in her left hand, cover them with her right hand and ask them,

"Where shall you best be blown? East, west, north or south?"

The seeds always whisper the direction into her feet.

"East," they say.

Euphoria will turn east, lift her right hand and blow gently on the seeds. They will swirl out of her palm and fly off on their own to plant themselves into prepared soil beds, burrowing their tiny selves at just the right depth. Every variety of seed is asked the same question in the same way and responds in this manner, until the entire Enchantment Garden has been planted.

The Three Sisters, Bean, Corn and Squash, group themselves together just as they have for the past four hundred years. Arugula, asparagus, cilantro, rosemary and parsley make a patchwork quilt alternating with tomatoes and peppers and cucumbers, their vines climbing around copper and crystal poles.

Sun kissed peaches and oranges, poppies and persimmons, beets and borage, cardamon and cantaloupes, lilacs and lettuce, mugwort and mangoes, chilies and chia seeds, mushrooms and mint, sweet grass and squash, pears and petunias, pansies and peonies, violets and vetiver, apples and anise, pomegranates and peas, rye and radicchio, walnuts and watercress, lemons and lavender, cabbage and chamomile, burdock and blueberry, delphinium and dandelion, yams and yarrow, peanuts and plums, ashwaganga and astragalus, ginger and grapes, horseradish and hawthorn berry, garlic and ginko, rhubarb and raspberry.

Euphoria sings her Flower Charms song as she walks through The Enchantment Garden, accompanied by honey bee drone, hummingbird wing buzz and the flutter of butterfly wings.

By mid summer all thirty-six varieties of New Witch Roses will have bloomed. That is the time when the Witchess Green are so thoroughly intoxicated by rose perfume and color, they barely are able to move their bodies for days at a time.

"FLOWER CHARMS"

Dandelion, Passion Flower, Violet, Rose
Geranium, Lavender, Cinnamon, Clove

Daffodil, Periwinkle, Cherry Blossom, Tulip
Sunflower, Marigold, Nasturtium, Sage

Rosemary, Delphinium, Chrysanthemum, Pine
Honeysuckle, Lemon Balm, Saffron, Tulsi

Gladiola, Apple Blossom, Lilac, Poppy
Iris, Lily, Pansy, Daisy

Morning Glory, Anemone, Jasmine, Ginger
Borage, Bergamot, Clover, Peony

***

The Witchess Calendar (pronounced Calandra)
Januarium
Februarium
Marchis
Aprilarium
Maytus
Junius
Jularium
Augustus
Septembrium
Octobrium
Novembrium
Decembrius

27

Adore In The Rain

Rooted to Lady Liberty's torch, Adore discovers the joy of the warm rains of Spring.

"Rain, rain, rain, rain, rain, rain, rain," he repeats like a mantra. "Every blade of grass, every leaf, every flower welcomes the rain. Even the edifices below, of stone and steel thirst for rain."

Adore is elated by his thoughts. They take form above his head, swirling and spinning their golden threads into the air.

"Angels do not know the elements as humans do. One must have a body to do that. I am thrilled to be cold and hot, wet and dry. Alive inside I feel the outside. What magnificence. Human beings too distracted by their toys, ignore the magic of their bodies. What sorrow to neglect these gifts."

Adore's heart begins to ache.

"And where is she, whom I close my eyes to see? She who rides upon the wind. Where does she go? Somewhere near, yet somewhere hidden."

Adore scans the horizon with his inner ear. He finally locates Euphoria's voice in the sky way above of Manhattan Isle.

"Ah, there she is. I hear her now."

28

Euphoria's Pretend Conversation

Euphoria's heart still beats fast for Adore. She has pretend conversations with him during her morning Sigil flight.
"Why are you called Euphoria?" Adore would ask.
"I was born with a Witchess gift, a Circle of Stars spinning in my eyes from the moment I opened them. That's what happens when a Witchess feels intense pleasure," I would reply.
Then I'd add,
"You haven't seen me at my best. Just wait. Next time I'll show you. I am very lucky in the clothes department.
Bella has kept every single garment worn by our ancestors since they first arrived in New Witch. She is so proud of their handiwork from making all their own garments.
When I was a child, Bella led me to a hidden room where I found piles of Lenape and Pilgrim children's clothes. She loved watching me dress up. As I grew older she gave me Edwardian dresses and shoes and then Victorian blouses with lace and ruffles and hats with plumes and gloves and pointy laced up boots.

She always made a history lesson of sorts, while introducing me to new clothing styles and we would spend time in our library reading plays and poems. Thanks to Great Grandmother Sparkle's opulent lifestyle, I have a stash of stunning beaded flapper dresses and fur lined velvet opera coats and every imaginable kind of ball gown to choose from. My favorite is my Victorian waistcoat and violet silk mini dress from the 60's. That's what I wore the other day when we met. Do you remember?"

Then Adore would say,

"I remember everything. You have the most beautiful thighs and Sapphire eyes I've ever seen."

Euphoria blushes all over, just imagining him saying that.

29

Emeraldine Meets Glorious

Soon after her arrival in New Witch, the skin on Emeraldine's face begins to crack, as if she has applied an egg white facial masque. Peeling off small pieces every day and gasping with delight at the fresh rosy golden skin below.

"Children here lose their baby teeth. So why wouldn't Angels lose their Angel skin. You are molting!" Euphoria teases her.

"It must be from laughing so much. It's making me grow new skin. I am becoming Witchess." Emeraldine says, grinning with new rosy cheeks.

"Not with those wings!" Euphoria pokes.

"They're looking perkier don't you think?" Emeraldine says spreading her wings full span.

"Yes they are. That's what happens when an Angel can't stop eating." Euphoria says laughing, blowing her a kiss as she leaves.

* * *

Prunella has offered to teach Emeraldine the Greens secret recipe for making Gem Stone Honey Jam using the Blueberries and Raspberries they gathered this morning.

Later that afternoon Glorious returns from work and heads into the kitchen where Prunella has been waiting for him. Clasping both of her paws together she announces,

"We are going to be bake some amazing bread," Prunella says, clasping both of her paws together. "I already soaked the grain in my new elixir, Celestial Cat. Just one bite of our bread and the codes will go straight into their bones."

Emeraldine mirrors Prunella's paw gesture.

Glorious remains in the doorway staring at Emeraldine, holding his breath for a beat or two.

"And who may I ask are you?" he asks dramatically.

"I'm Emeraldine," she squeals, bobbing up and down causing the dishes to rattle.

"Oops, sorry, I'm so excited to meet you," her voice quivering.

"You're one of them. So it's not just a hoax, OK. So tell me what exactly is your agenda on Earth?" Glorious says narrowing his eyes.

"I don't have one. I fell into a tree in your forest. Your sister found me," Emeraldine says with great pride.

"Look at the gem jams we just made Glorious." Prunella interjects, pointing to several sparkling jars on the kitchen counter.

"Wow, they are beautiful," Glorious switches gears, relaxing he smiles at Emeraldine.

Prunella decides to leave the two of them alone and quietly exits through her cat door.

"I see they've already got you on our kitchen team. I've got to start prepping for the Cafe tomorrow." Glorious says slyly.

"May I help?" Emeraldine asks, going for the bait.

It is already obvious to Glorious, that she is smitten with him. But as curious as he is about Emeraldine, she also frightens him. He keeps a friendly distance and walks the edges of the kitchen.

"Of course you may. I will show you how to make the most mouth watering pie crusts from scratch," he says.

Glorious heads over to a row of large rainbow colored steel bins are against the pantry wall.

"Here's where we keep our flours."

Glorious turns and speaks to the house.

"Bella, four large mixing bowls please," he says.

Bella obliges opening the lower cupboard doors and four huge steel mixing bowls come sliding across the kitchen floor. One red, one blue, one green and one yellow.

Glorious points to four colored flour bins and then to each of the colored bowls.

"Red is for the Rice, Blue is for the Buckwheat, Green is for the Almond, Yellow is for the Chickpea."

Emeraldine mimics his gestures and intonation exactly.

"Red is for the Rice, Blue is for the Buckwheat, Green is for the Almond, Yellow is for the Chickpea."

"Excellent! Now, you go ahead and put four cups of each flour in its matching colored bowl. Here's the measuring cup." Glorious hands her a huge magnificent crystal measuring cup.

Emeraldine is so excited she cannot stop bobbing up and down, and while measuring the flour much of it goes flying into the air in a fine mist, landing all over her hair and face. By the time she is done filling each bowl, Emeraldine is completely covered in flour.

Glorious tries not to laugh at her, but finally he loses it. Emeraldine loses it as well and sneezes and laughs heartily along with him.

Prunella comes back into the kitchen with a bunch of catnip.

"Don't you worry Emeraldine. I'll get all that flour off you. We never waste good flour. I can use it for my cat nippy rolls."

Prunella puts a large sheet of wax paper on the floor and directs Emeraldine to stand in the center of it.

"Now shake like this," she instructs Emeraldine. Sitting up on her hind legs, Prunella sways her long lavender torso and starts to shimmy like Euphoria often does.

Emeraldine imitates her. While most of the flour goes flying into the air, plenty of it lands on the wax paper which Prunella then drags back over to her kitchen in the corner.

"A purrfect amount for my rolls," Prunella begins to sing:

> *Crumbs from buns and left over honey*
> *Drops from oil and drips of sauce*
> *All good things my Witchess leave behind*
> *When the cooking's done and the eating is over*
> *Nice for mice and ants and birds*
> *But a cat such as I*
> *I grabs them first*
> *To sweeten and savor*
> *My culinary creations*

Meanwhile, Glorious has been blending almond flour, pecans, flax seeds, honey, lemon juice and coconut oil for Fruit Pie crust.

Rice flour, pine nuts, dill, pink salt, garlic powder and olive oil for the Shroom Pie crust.

Buckwheat flour, pumpkin seeds, cumin, coriander and macadamia nut oil for Veggie Pie crust.

Chickpea flour, cashews, black sesame seeds, rosemary, sage and pistachio oil for Bean Pie crust.

Emeraldine can barely breathe just watching him. She hasn't moved for several minutes, standing perfectly still, totally mesmerized by the dance of his hands, his fingers beautifully articulating the precise selection and measurement of each ingredient.

In addition miraculous things are appearing and disappearing via Bella's assistance. Bella adding more ovens and disappearing them as needed, making room for additional counter space. In no time the kitchen is filled with the most delicious aroma of twelve perfectly scrumptious pie crusts.

"We will leave them here to cool for the night," Glorious says looking at Prunella, who is already looking guilty.

"Prunella, do I need to put a 'Do Not Disturb' sign on the table?" Glorious teases.

"I wouldn't dream of touching them, while I'm awake. But as we both know, I do, upon occasion, have been known to walk in my sleep," she says grinning slyly.

"Then lock your door," Glorious says, shaking his finger.

He turns to Emeraldine,

"Emeraldine, it has been a pleasure meeting you. Thank you for all your help this evening."

Emeraldine blushes from head to toe,

"Anytime Glorious."

Glorious gives her a slight bow,

"Good Night."

Emeraldine can barely speak.

"Goodnight," she whispers.

30

Glorious Kisses Emeraldine

Glorious is not attracted to Emeraldine. He is put off by her bouncy moon walk, her high pitch squeals, her cooing bird like voice, but most of all, by her big pale blue opalescent wings.

"They are of no use, I wish you could take them off like a sweater," he says next evening.

They are gathering herbs in the Enchantment Garden. The moon is bright, the stars are dazzling and Emeraldine completely smitten has baked him his favorite Shroom pie for dinner. As much as Glorious loves Emeraldine's culinary attention, he has not warmed up to anything romantic between them.

Standing in the moonlight together he senses her hunger for his affection. More out of curiosity than desire, Glorious kisses her. And wham! Kissing Emeraldine is like blasting off into space. Energy goes roaring up the base of his tailbone to the crown of his head with a blinding light that explodes into a thousand stars.

Emeraldine, on the other hand, pushes Glorious away.

"Ouch, that burns," she yells.

Upset and confused by the pain, she rushes back into the house. Stunned, Glorious collapses on the grass and goes out like a light.

31

Euphoria Coaches Emeraldine

Next morning Glorious is back to himself.
"She's way too big and feathery for me," he complains to Euphoria, who suggests he and Emeraldine make a good couple.

"You know me. I like women who have dark edges, neurotic and exotic," he says laughing.

Euphoria decides to coach Emeraldine on getting Dark Edges.

***

Since her arrival in New Witch, Emeraldine has been wearing the same long white cotton and lace gown. It mysteriously never wrinkles or gets dirty, regardless what she is doing.

Out of consideration, Euphoria has resisted asking her why.

Motivated now, Euphoria suggests Emeraldine try on her purple Victorian dress, just for fun, but Emeraldine refuses.

"My Angel gown is more than a dress," she says in a cryptic tone and leaves it at that.

Moving on to Glorious's next caveat, Euphoria wonders how to help Emeraldine from bouncing up and down so much.

She fetches a pair of her clunky Doc Martin boots and insists Emeraldine put them on. They appear to do the trick! Progress.

Next, she instructs Emeraldine on how to go about lowering her vocal register when speaking.

"Try imitating how Grandmother Promise's voice sounds. Say *Hello Glorious* from down here, pointing to her belly button.

Emeraldine tries over and over but her voice doesn't seem to get any lower, so they skip that idea. Drastic measures are needed now.

Terrified, Euphoria attempts to trim Emeraldine's wings, but to her relief they instantly grow back.

Her last hope, she reluctantly dyes Emeraldine's hair black. But, alas, the dye simply does not take.

Crest fallen, Emeraldine confesses,

"When Glorious kissed me, it burned me inside here," she says placing her hands on her heart.

"I want to give myself to him, but my wings get in the way. I want to merge with him so that wherever I go, he goes with me," Emeraldine says passionately.

"Oh dear. You are one smashed Angel. Be patient with him. Glorious is elusive when it comes to women. Besides, I still have so much to share with you. As does Witch Hazel and Grandmother Promise and Bella and Prunella. We love you just the way you are," Euphoria adds, hoping to comfort her.

It appears to work. Emeraldine takes a deep breath, spreads her wings wide and proud. Tossing her pale blue hair with both hands, she strikes a pose and sings,

"You Make Me Feel Like A Natural Woman."

They both laugh hysterically and hug.

32

Angels Don't Sleep

Emeraldine pretends to go to bed at night, but Angels don't sleep. She waits until all three of the Greens are merrily snoring away, then goes bouncing across her bedroom and down stairs to explore more of Bella. Bella does not sleep either and is thrilled to have her company. "Bella, you have such a wondrous appetite for the fantastic," Emeraldine whispers, having just discovered another new room. This room appears to be floating, its walls covered in pale blue and white flowers and its floor a lake made of mother of pearl. A tall chifferobe is standing right in the center, its doors flung wide open. It is filled with gowns. Gowns especially made for someone with wings. Strapless gowns in the palest of blue and deepest of emerald silk. Excellent for showing off Emeraldine's beautiful shoulders. Draped over the mirror is a long white fur wrap. Emeraldine can not resist stroking it. Suddenly she panics, recalling how many rabbits' must have given up their lives for this garment. Bella can hear her heart and slides its label across the floor to her feet. It says ' No Animals Harmed In The Making Of This Garment.'

"How is that possible? " Emeraldine ask.

Bella flips the label over, 'Made by MAGIC.' Emeraldine dissolves into giggles, kisses the label and twirls around, her wings sending a breeze across the room.

"Oh Bella you are the best house ever." Bella is on a roll...She leads Emeraldine back upstairs to her bedroom and opens a mysterious descending staircase right in the center of the floor. A chorus of frog song rising from beneath beckons Emeraldine to descend its shallow stone steps. She finds herself in an ancient grotto of emerald water mirroring the starry heavens above. It is an Angel Pool. Emeraldine immerses herself. Floating on her back, her wings fully extended upon the star dappled waters. Her pale blue hair spread out in a halo around her head. She sings:

SONG
" ANGEL TEAR SOUP "

Some broths are made of Stones
Some broths are made of Bones
Some soups have Beans or Meat
Some soups are Bitter or Sweet
My Tears are made from the Dust of Stars
My soups will make you Laugh and Weep
My soups have the power to Heal
My soups can lift your Heart,
Give you the courage to Feel
Teach you to hold on and Never Give Up
Some broths are made of Light
Some broths are made of Fire
My Tears are made from the Dust of Stars

33

Angels Effect On Earth

The Angels have stopped the world. No one can tear their eyes away from the skies. Media headlines are calling it a Zeigfield Follies from Heaven. Streets are buzzing with speculations. If this were an alien invasion, would it behave like this?

Malachiah Davis is eleven years old and lives in the Bronx. His six year old sister Melody died in a fire last year.

Three days ago Malachiah discovered an Angel next to the fire hydrant in front of his apartment building. He is convinced the Angel is his sister Melody. The Angel looks exactly like her, but older he says. His parents agree. The resemblance has been quite unnerving for them.

Since then Malachiah refuses to attend school. Instead he has set up camp beside the Angel and takes all his meals outside as well. He has placed photos of his sister and arranged Melody's old toys and dolls in a shrine around the Angel.

Malachiah and Angel Melody have written a song together. Malachiah sings it when anyone stops to look at the photos of his sister and acknowledges the resemblance to the Angel Melody.

SONG
HUMAN ANGEL

Human Angel, Human Angel
Reach In My Heart
Speak To My Soul

Human Angel, Human Angel
The Time Has Come
Welcome Home

Help Me Feel The Light
And The Love
That I Am
Help Me Live This Truth
In The World

Human Angel, Human Angel
Heal Thru My Arms
Breathe With My Soul

Human Angel, Human Angel
Welcome Home

34

Crone Glamour Podcast

Promise is back in her studio ruffling through her notes for today's podcast. She adjusts her microphone and jumps right in.

"Welcome back my lovelies. Time for Crone Glamour with yours truly, Clitasaurus ~ Dinosaur Priestess Talk Show Hostess.

As many of you have already noticed, aging does nothing to stop me. In fact the brew of me just keeps getting stronger and stronger. I am sweeter, meaner and sharper in all the right places. Every year adds more flavor. Every year there's more of me to savor.

Don't be fooled by age. Skin may sag and wrinkle. Muscles lose tone, bones may shrivel. Yet another invincible power begins to stir within, a force to be reckoned with my lovelies, a force indeed.

Aging is an opportunity to earn the art of self regeneration. We are on our way DOWN. No more growing UP, we are growing DOWN. We get to see where we've been. We get to slow down and look around. We get to let it all go and make it up as we go.

Crone Glamour is high fashion for women over the hill and over themselves. Every day we nourish and flourish. Dip those dry petals in honey and oil. Steep those dry bones in salt and mud.

"Hydrate, saturate, exfoliate, celebrate, praise your body, pray your body, heaven is within. Wisdom is so misunderstood. Wisdom accumulates and disperses through action. Believing Wisdom is a compensation prize for aging is utterly ridiculous! Older women are not necessarily wiser than their younger counterparts.

As for myself, Wisdom is Glamour. It is ongoing and my desire for it increases daily. Crone Glamour says, I am the same but so much more so. Concentrated, potent, a walking talking tincture, a deeply steeped infusion, a super food wonder bar.

The older I get, the more marvelous I am. The more galactic sparkle I have," Clitasaurus pauses, gyrating in her chair.

"My lovelies, as we enter the realm of Crone Glamour, there are several common misconceptions I would like to address.

First and foremost Glamour, as known throughout the ages, has been driven by healthy hormonal impulses, to enhance points of attraction between consenting parties for the purposes of pro creation and pleasure. But then monetized, fostering the ridiculous assumption women of seniority will all jump off a cliff's edge into a ravine of self loathing. We will do anything to not be wrinkled and sagging, least our faces be frozen in a grimace of envy at every woman younger than ourselves. But, Guess What? We DID NOT! WE DO NOT!! WE WILL NOT!!! We don't give a hoot's ass about how we look to other people anymore, now do we? We Care About How We Feel Inside!!! " Clitasaurus stretches these last words.

We dance for the love of our limbs moving, we flex our Crone Glamour bones with our Crone Glamour muscles. Stretch our Crone Glamour spine for the sheer supple strength and sensation it gives us. We feel alive on the inside. We hear ourselves, we see ourselves, we know who we are, what we are, why we are. No longer posing and prancing to arouse anyone. We arouse ourselves, for ourselves."

Clitasaurus pauses to sip her elderberry tea infused with Sapphire Gem Stone Honey. Marveling at the starry sky swirling in her tea cup before she continues speaking.

"I owe my feisty, lusty, tenacious nature to my ancestors. My lineage can be traced back to the native people of Manhattan Isle. I am Lenape on my Great Great Grandfather's side and Dutch on my Great Great Grandmother's. Having both blood lines flowing through my veins has opened my eyes to many things hidden.

Four hundred years ago, Lenape women were revered as heads of their households. They ruled over their homes and their land. They taught their children how to handle all their own legal affairs, including whatever trade treaties needed to be signed. The real information about these women has been omitted from our public schools. The Dutch women of New Amsterdam retained their own last name when they married. Prenuptial agreements were standard in New Amsterdam. They gave Dutch women significant autonomy and enabled those with money and property to keep their wealth after they married. If a woman was unmarried, she was treated under the law just as a man would be treated. When she married, she could choose to marry according to 'manus' or according to 'usus'. If she chose 'manus', she granted her husband marital power over her. But if a she chose 'usus', she rejected marital power, and thereby retained all her own property. Dutch law also afforded women to engage freely in business and practice medicine as midwives and physicians. It was only when English law replaced Dutch law, that women's rights eroded and then finally disappeared for centuries.

On a more personal level I would like to add that when people use the word "Indian" or "Native American" they are unconsciously consenting to being deeply misguided. They have cut the root. Separated the stem. Destroyed possibility of its fruits existence. You cannot separate human beings from the Earth. It's not about where you force them to live. It's all about how you force them to stop living. Stop speaking, stop moving, stop caring, stop being cared for. The Earth cares for us, if we do not prevent it from doing what it does naturally.

So much to ponder my lovelies. To be continued. Until next time! Steep deep. Bask in the light, CRONE GLAMOUR!!!"

Promise exhales and smiles with satisfaction.

Rising from her throne she announces loudly and clearly so Onyx can hear her,

"Best part of the day is being with Onyx."

Looking up at the ceiling, she yells,

"I'll be right up!"

Promise starts singing while climbing up the stairs to the roof,

Oh Glory Bee
Oh Glory Bee
Mama Gave Me
My Very Own Angel
Mama Gave Me
Mama Gave Me
Mama Gave Me
My Very Own Angel

35

Lenape Heritage Festival

Grandmother Promise has made a banner for the Festival's auction. It is sixteen feet wide and nine feet high of pure indigo silk, depicting nature's bounty flowing from Heaven to Earth. Every detail is handmade from wool, dried herbs, flowers, moss, twine and tiny gem stones. The effect is dazzling to behold. All the auction's proceeds go to the Lenape Foundation, dedicated to preserving the Lenape language, history and culture for generations to come.

Euphoria has prepared amber glass colored bottles of Lenape Spirit Potion, tinctures of white pine needles, dried mushrooms and Gemstone Honey. Grandmother Promise has prepared Bee Lenape Gemstone Honey in cobalt blue glass jars decorated with tiny corn husk dolls. Glorious has prepared his Three Sisters - Soup, Pudding and Pies made from Corn, Beans and Squash, served in hand made clay bowls customers get to keep. Each bowl is inscribed with a Lenape word they can look up at the Lenape Talking Dictionary Booth. Made by the Askaskwe tribe, Welsit Hakihakan, New York. The Lenape word for Green is *Askaskwe*, Garden is *Hakihakan,* Enchanted is *Welsit.*

ANGELS AND WITCHESS - 83

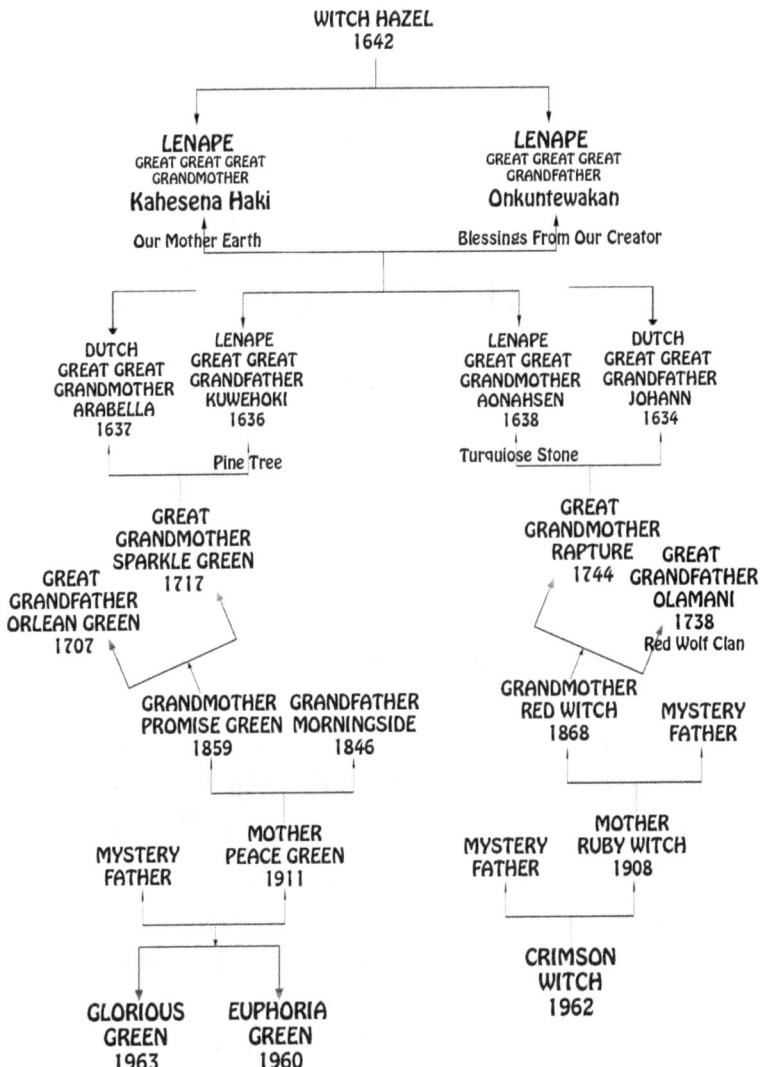

36

Emeraldine & Euphoria In The Enchantment Garden

Euphoria is tutoring Emeraldine in the Enchantment Garden while gathering purple sage, parsley, cilantro and thyme. "The Enchantment Garden, like everything in New Witch, is an ongoing evolving manifestation of Nature's intelligence. I know for many people it is strange to imagine that cucumbers learn whilst they ripen on the vine. But they do. Most plants talk while they are learning. Sometimes they sing. If only people could hear their vegetables sing, what a different world it would be. "

Emeraldine leans over to listen to a cucumber vine nearby.

"The Bees are our greatest teachers. We have our own unique species in New Witch. If you were to look at them under microscope you'd see tiny circles of stars rotating inside their eyes, just like mine. Only for Bees, the direction of rotation and speed communicates specific information between them and each plant."

"How does one become a Witchess?" Emeraldine asks.

"I am not a Witchess by choice," confesses Euphoria.

"I did not plan for this kind of life, nor did I train for it. I was born into it. The first thing I remember were two amethyst pools with stars spinning slowly inside them. Those were my mother's eyes. Her name was Peace Green.

I started levitating while I was still an infant. One day mother found me crawling on the ceiling. After that she attached a net over my crib to keep me from floating out the window.

Later Grandmother Promise made a weighted harness out of deerskin and rocks to which I was firmly strapped in, against my will of course. I cannot imagine how my mother put up with my constant wailing in her ears. Grandmother says, Peace just sang louder than my screams and eventually I stopped screaming and started singing along with her.

My mother sang until her very last breath. Her bones are buried in the Ancestor Circle, not far from Witch Hazel's tree. When Witchess die, we do not mourn. We carry on brighter and stronger. We become more than ourselves. We Witchess say, 'Long Live My Mother in Me.'"

Euphoria pauses, then looks deeply into Emeraldine's eyes.

"Emeraldine, are Angels born?"

Emeraldine says thoughtfully,

"I was never born. Nor will I ever die. But perhaps, by my being here, where dying is allowed, I will die."

"Why do you have wings?" Euphoria asks.

"I really don't have wings," Emeraldine confesses.

"This is your idea of me, not mine. Remember, I am as you have chosen to see me. I would not have given myself wings. You can fly and you don't have wings. How do you fly?"

"I was born knowing I could. But I had lessons as well, similar to ballet. Foot positions, arm movements, hand gestures and back bends. It took a great deal of practice learning to coordinate my limbs while navigating through the atmosphere. I learned to harmonize my body with the wind, with all its varying pressures and speeds. It's much more than merely dancing in the air."

Euphoria has been switching positions to demonstrate several ballet bar type foot exercises.

"My cousin, Crimson Witch lives on Manhattan Isle full time. She is a professional dancer and runs The Red Shoes Dance Studio. She trains Sky Dancers," Euphoria says proudly.

Emeraldine's eyes brighten,

"Could I be a Sky Dancer?" Emeraldine asks.

"Crimson Witch takes no prisoners. She is notorious for dismissing students for lack of talent or ability. She can be brutal in that respect. Hard on frail egos, but the end result is a stellar dance troupe that outshines all the rest of them. You'll never look up at the sky the same way again, after seeing her Sky Dancers up there."

Sensing Emeraldine's disappointment at not being able to fly, Euphoria tries consoling her.

"There are many ways to fly Emeraldine. You can fly with your eyes on the wings of sight. You can fly with your tongue on the wings of taste. You can fly with your ears on the wings of sound. You can fly with your fingers on the wings of touch. You can fly with your nose on the wings of scent, fly upon fragrances everywhere found. Dive deep into all your senses Emeraldine and worlds upon worlds will unfold. Until that day comes when your wings work again, there is much flying to be done right here, just being with us in New Witch."

Emeraldine takes a deep breath and smiles, thinking to herself,

"Just you wait Euphoria. I will fly again. And soon."

37

Euphoria's Herbalarium

Euphoria leads Emeraldine down a narrow stone path, past the rose garden, past the Bee Hives, deeper into New Witch forest. Emeraldine has never explored this part of the forest. There are enormous Redwood trees here and the forest floor is smothered in ancient moss, lush ferns and multi colored mushrooms.

Finally they reach a clearing. The sunlight seems to be playing tricks, reflecting the surrounding forest like a mirror creating a halo of shimmering prisms, bouncing tiny rainbows in the air.

Upon getting closer, Emeraldine sees it is a sparkling geodesic dome made entirely out of crystal . There are eight round windows spiraling counter clockwise to open and clockwise to close as if they are breathing. Euphoria turns to Emeraldine and waving her arms in a grand flourish she curtsies,

"My Herbalarium," she says.

She removes a tiny gold key from the chatelaine attached to her belt, and inserts it into a lock on a door barely visible. The most heavenly fragrances come pouring out at the threshold.

Instantly intoxicated Emeraldine remains standing in the doorway, eyes closed, unable to move. Euphoria realizes what is happening and laughs.

"You're getting drunk Emeraldine. Come inside," says pushing her inside the Herbalarium.

It is a place is unlike anything else in New Witch. The intensity of light pouring into the Herbalarium is supra-natural. It is like being in a Light Ship.

Center stage is an elaborate perfumer's organ made entirely of alabaster. Its shelves are lined with hundreds of perfume bottles, in all sorts of fantastic shapes and sizes. They create a kaleidoscope of patterns throughout the chamber. The effect is so dazzling that Emeraldine has been rendered speechless.

The Herbalarium has been aligned to Earth's cardinal directions. In the South there is a white marble fireplace with two gleaming copper cauldrons. Above the fireplace, an ancient broom floats mid air. Its handle made of Diamond and its broom grass made of spun Gold.

Above the broom is a portrait of Great Grandmother Sparkle and Great Grandfather Orlean, surrounded by three children. The baby on Sparkle's lap is Grandmother Promise.

In the East there are alabaster counters and shelves, holding glassware and pottery, stacks of drying trays, screen frames, mortars, pestles and other strange tools and vessels.

In the West is an enormous copper sink with water that flows down through two vertical crystal pipes from the dome's ceiling. More alabaster shelves lined with jars full of herbs and spices on either side of the sink.

In the North, are two Victorian settees covered in silk velvet. A lavish tea set waiting on a low oval table between them.

Emeraldine bounces gracefully and cautiously around the perfume organ, careful not to upset anything, goes to sit on the settee.

Raspberry tea is steeping in the Emerald tea pot and two spoonfuls of Blueberry Honey are inside two Emerald tea cups. There is a cookie jar on the table made of Amethyst in the shape of a cat looking very much like Prunella. Emeraldine peers inside. Only one cookie left. Clearly evidence that Euphoria's sweet tooth has been indulged in as of late. On cue, Euphoria fills the cookie jar with fresh violet pecan shortbread and lemon poppy seed cookies, then pours Emeraldine a cup of tea.

"When I'm not out in the forest gathering mushrooms, or preparing herbs and spices for Faery Cakes, this is where I spend most of my time," she says.

Emeraldine reclines in the curve of the settee.

"Why would you ever want to leave the Herbalarium?" she says and sighs.

"Here is where I prefer to be. But my higher purpose is to share what I create here with the world. Potion making is a serious art. It requires devotion, integrity and patience. To that end, I test everything on myself first. If it doesn't kill me, I try it on Glorious. If it doesn't kill him, I try it on Grandmother Promise," Euphoria says laughing.

"Only then, after I verify the results are safe and beneficial, will I ask for volunteers from my students."

Euphoria has been straightening up her potion making counter while speaking. When she looks up she sees Emeraldine has fallen asleep on the settee.

"Oh my goodness! Look at that. This is a good sign," Euphoria says, looking up at the ghost of Great Grandmother Sparkle, who has been waltzing high above their heads, since they first entered the Herbalarium.

38

Great Grandmother Sparkle

Euphoria sits in the twilight waiting for Emeraldine to wake up from her unexpected afternoon nap. With Sparkle's ghost floating about, Euphoria has kept busy dusting perfume bottles from Sparkle's collection from France and Spain and Morocco.

When Emeraldine wakes up, Euphoria makes a fresh pot of peppermint tea and decides to share the story of her Great Grandmother, knowing it will please Sparkle's ghost to hear it. Curling up on the settee across from Emeraldine she begins.

"Centuries ago, our Great Grandmother Sparkle Green traveled to Paris in hope of becoming an actress. There she met and fell in love with the conductor Maestro Orlean Verte. After they married Sparkle took the stage name Sapienta Verte.

The Vertes started a theater company, *Le Theatre Du Sapienta*. It became notorious for its fantastical, numinous stage effects. Their performers could float throughout the theater like spectral beings, gliding onto the stage as if skating on ice. Their ethereal style became the thrall of fashion everywhere in Paris. Shoe makers seeking to imitate these effects began adding tiny wheels to leather boots and evening slippers. Tailors added long trailing capes to conceal the wheels. Throughout the streets of Paris, women and men went bumping into one another, knocking over carts, bruising knees and twisting ankles. The Mayor finally banned the sale of such outlandish footwear. Hoping to put an end to this fashion obsession, he fined all the shops that sold them.

Madame Sapienta was forced to include a liability footnote in her Theater Company's program, stating *Le Theatre Du Sapienta* takes no responsibility whatsoever for anyone attempting to imitate their choreography, neither inside nor outside the Theater's premises. In her interviews with the French press, she insisted,

"Our actors are trained professionals, licensed and contracted to perform these movements."

Of course that was not the whole truth. All her actors were regularly given Madame Sapienta's levitation potion. They did so willingly, just as one might consent to undergo hypnosis today.

In those days, especially in countries such as France, Potions were just a matter of course.

Sadly, *Le Theatre Du Sapienta* lasted just a brief span of fifty years. Coming naturally to an end when Madame Sapienta and Maestro Orlean decided they wanted to raise a family of their own.

They promptly returned to New Witch and did just that." Euphoria finishes and looks at Emeraldine with a big grin. Emeraldine has been watching Great Grandmother Sparkle's ghost do a somersault above her head and then slip seamlessly back into the family portrait. The effect was so perfectly timed to those last few words, she wonders if Euphoria is the one responsible for producing the illusion for her to see at that very moment.

"Did you just do that?" She asks. Euphoria simply shakes her head no.

39

Promise & Onyx Girl Talk

Promise is on the roof standing next to Onyx with her eyes closed and her arms extended in a Qi Gong pose.
"How is it possible for you to be inside my mind?" she asks.

"I am not inside your mind. I am a reflection of your soul," Onyx replies.

"Why do you make me weep so easily?" Promise asks.

"You weep easily because you are easily distracted and I bring you back to yourself. You are addicted to being on stage, always needing an audience. You love glamour and drama. Old as you are, you have the desires of a child," Onyx replies.

Promise drops down to the floor, laughing hysterically like a teenage girl.

"Oh Onyx, I love how you see right through me. You are my Celestial Guru, my Mother of Stars, my Queen of Heaven," she declares adoringly, shifting on to her knees and bowing in worship.

Onyx rolls her eyes. "Now wait a minute. Do not worship me. I am that part of you that reflects your own light, your own wisdom. I am merely a mirror for you to see yourself more clearly.

Own your truth, it's all you. Now, don't we have some work to do today?" Onyx reminds her.

"Yes, of course. Where were we? My new podcast needs a theme song."

"Yes it does. How about this?" Onyx begins to rap:

A Mindful Rap

Your vagina is a flower, it contains a secret power
If you choose it, You can use it, Let it guide you
Your vagina has a mind, doesn't like it when you lie
Wants the truth, Chooses life, Let it show you
Are you brave enough to listen?
Are you smart enough to let it in?
RU Vagina? RU Vagina Mindful?
It's a touchy situation, passed down every generation
Mothers wishing they could change it
Then retreat from explaining
All the goodness you were born with
All the love and satisfaction
Healthy pleasure takes some practice
No shame, No fatal attraction
RU Vagina? RU Vagina Mindful

Promise is clearly impressed.

"Onyx, I just realized I know nothing about you." she says.

"I am as you choose to see me," Onyx replies.

"But there must be something inside you, that is yours and yours alone," Promise insists.

"That is your vision, not mine," Onyx answers gently.

"What is your vision?" Promise persists.

"My vision is to respond. I perceive what is being asked of me and I respond without question," Onyx explains.

Closing her eyes Onyx begins to sing:

SONG
"This Is What An Angel Does"

This is what an Angel does
Like the Rain
That quenches the thirst of a Rose
We Fall
Like the Wind
That carries the seeds through the Air
We Flow
Like the Earth that gives Birth
To all that wants to Grow
We Embrace and we Hold
And then we Let Go

This is what an Angel does

You choose where and when and why
You choose how and which desire
We show up, when you give up
When you get lost
When you lose hope
When you go too far, Or not far enough

This is what an Angel does
And then we Let Go

40

Adore Hears Onyx Singing

Adore still hears Euphoria shrieking long after she has gone.
"My eyes were too strong. My words were too strong."
Adore begins to question his purpose.
"How do I serve her? She wants me to choose her. No one has ever asked that of me. How do I choose? I don't know how to choose. Why is that? Where is inside of me, is the I that chooses?
Suddenly Adore hears Onyx singing. He sings along with her.

> *You choose where and when and why*
> *You choose how and which desire*
> *We show up when you give up*
> *When you get lost*
> *When you lose hope*
> *When you go too far Or not far enough*
>
> *This is what an Angel does*
> *Then we Let Go*

41

Euphoria & Glorious About the Met

Euphoria is coasting along 5th avenue, talking to herself as usual on her Sigil flight over Manhattan Isle each morning.

"I've seen this island go from magic to manic, killing the very spirit of its purpose. And now as if our prayers have been answered, the Angels are here dotting this digitized landscape, breaking all the illusions of control. Human beings control nothing."

Euphoria's laughter goes bouncing between the skyscrapers in a rippling echo. The city has been unusually quiet for several days. For many people it has been a time of great reflection. Even traffic has a meditative drone. Subways sounding softer, almost muted.

Later that afternoon Euphoria and Glorious cleaning up after Faery Cakes lunch rush.

"Pearl told me she heard that The Metropolitan Museum of Art is drooling over the idea of taking credit for the presence of the Angels and presenting them as an exhibition and charging people to see them. Can you believe that?" Euphoria says in disbelief.

"That will never happen." Glorious responds defiantly.

"Of course not. She said one of the Museum's employees tried roping off an area where an Angel was standing, they heard the Angel's voice exploded inside their head, screaming "STOP!" It freaked them out so bad they ran away and refused to go back. I'm sure that will put an end to that idea." Euphoria says, laughing.

Glorious face lights up,

"Similar things are happening all over the world. So far, no one has been able to move, control or influence the Angels in any way. They've tried setting them on fire, pulling them with trucks and chains, and even blowing them up. Nothing works. No power has over ridden their Celestial stand on Earth," he says, victoriously.

42

Emeraldine's Tears

Ever since Glorious kissed her Emeraldine has spent every night below her bedroom in the grotto, floating in the Angel Pool, staring into the dark velvet sky smothered in stars and weeping.

Weeping for the joy of being in a body. Weeping for wanting Glorious and weeping for the sorrow of his not wanting her.

Euphoria knows Emeraldine needs to sort these things out on her own, so she has given her lots of space and privacy to do so.

Several days pass and then Euphoria wakes in the middle of the night, knowing now is the right time to check on Emeraldine.

"Prunella, have you seen Emeraldine tonight?" She asks.

"Ask Bella," Prunella answers in her sleep.

"Bella, have you seen Emeraldine tonight?"

Bella lights the candle on the vanity table and sends it floating across the room, indicating Euphoria should follow.

The candle goes flickering into Emeraldine's bedroom and stops in the center of the room. Euphoria sees there is a descending staircase in the floor and hears Emeraldine weeping somewhere below.

Tiptoeing quietly down the stairs she discovers the grotto with Emeraldine sitting on a very large rock at the edge of the water.

"What is this?" Euphoria whispers.

Emeraldine looks up and smiles.

"I was hoping you would find me," she says.

There are huge sparkling diamond sized tears streaming down Emeraldine's face. They have been collecting in her lap and spilling down her gown, gathering around her feet.

"Emeraldine, look at your tears. They're sparkling stars."

Instantly an idea flashes across Euphoria's mind.

"Emeraldine, would you mind if I gather some of your tears?"

Emeraldine looks down at her tears and smiles.

"I don't mind," she says.

"Don't move. I'll be right back," Euphoria says, flying back up the staircase.

She returns in no time with a large wooden bucket and ladle and begins scooping up Emeraldine's tears as fast as she can. When the bucket is completely full, Euphoria kisses Emeraldine on both of her wet cheeks and says,

"Emeraldine, I will be in the Herbalarium if you need me."

Euphoria flies into the forest with the bucket of Angel tears, glowing like a huge fire fly.

43

Euphoria Experiments

Having filled several jars with Emeraldine's Tears, Euphoria's mind is in a whirl with an idea as to what she should do with them. Over the centuries every generation of the Green family has delighted in the art of cross pollinating roses grown in the Enchantment Garden. With so many varieties at her disposal Euphoria has dedicated an entire wall to Roses. Jars after jar of Rose Petals, Rose Tinctures, Rose Waters, Rose Sugars Rose Lotions, Rose Oils and most amazing Rose Honey glistening in hues of cherry, peach, pink and lilac. It is a staggering sight to behold.

"I can already feel the power of Emeraldine's Tears," she says holding one jar up to the sunlight pouring into the Herbalarium. Euphoria calms down knowing this is a supreme sacred moment.

"I thank Emeraldine for giving me these Angel Tears. You are a gift from Emeraldine's heart. So I ask you now to guide me and reveal to me what is your desire? Holy Spirit alive within these Angel Tears, show me where you want to go? "

Euphoria closes her eyes and waits, letting the Angel Tears point the way. They rise up from the table and pull Euphoria's hands to her heart.

"To me you wish to go?"

Even before she finishes her question, an Angel Tear ejects itself in a single drop into her open mouth. Euphoria gulps it down.

"Wow!!! One drop feels like a mouthful went down my throat."

Within moments she is totally over come with raw emotion. Retreating to her favorite armchair she curls up and starts wailing like a new born baby.

"From whence this tidal wave of sorrow come?" she cries.

Then continues sobbing. Muscles pulling deep within her womb, then into her loins, then back up into her guts and chest, behind every rib and both shoulder blades.

"Totally Euphoric!" she screams out.

She suddenly hears the Angel Tears speaking inside her heart,

"To know thyself in fullness, where every morsel of being contracts and spills its water is how to let the light in."

Several hours later Euphoria is completely rung out and falls into a very, very, deep, deep sleep.

When she wakes up it is twilight. Eagerly she proceeds asking the Angel Tears to select a partner among her Rose Tinctures. The Angel Tears pull her over to the jar marked Terra Red. They begin swirling clockwise emitting a high pitched ringing sound that to Euphoria's ears can only mean yes this one.

Euphoria removes Terra Red from the shelf and places it reverently on her work table. Terra Red is the first Rose tincture ever made in New Witch. It is several hundred years old and most likely brewed by Witch Hazel herself.

Again Euphoria asks the Angel Tears if there is any other Rose they would like to join with.

The Angel Tears pull her quickly to the left middle shelf and stop in front of a jar marked Blue Bell.

"Oh my goodness, I am honored, my very own variation and one of my favorites." Removing Blue Bell and placing it next to Terra Rose on her work table, "This is going to be amazing, I can feel it already, " Euphoria is now trembling with excitement.

"Okay. Which one do we begin with?" she asks placing the Angel Tears between the two Rose tinctures. The Angel Tears move to Terra Red first. Euphoria adds one drop of Terra Red to one drop of Angel Tears in a tiny crystal dish and holds her breath. Watching Terra Red swirl into the Angel Tear is like watching the birth of a Galaxy. Spiraling microscopic stars systems forming in pools of ruby red plasma. The sight of this potion begs being taken into one's mouth. Euphoria cannot resist. She lifts the tiny dish and tilts it over her tongue.

"Whooooo!!!! "

Euphoria's eyes growing wider as her Circle of Star Eyes spin so fast them become a circle of light. Waves upon waves of ecstatic bliss wash over her. Euphoria goes writhing onto the floor, lost in a vision that she is floating in sea made of sparkling roses. The fragrance is so intense, it puts her to sleep.

She wakes up next morning from something tickling the inside of her right wrist. The skin has broken and is bubbling. The most amazing thing is happening. A cluster of tiny rosebuds are emerging. They are growing straight out of her wrist. Euphoria is stunned, her jaw drops in disbelief.

"How is this possible? And there's no pain?"

Emeraldine has been standing in the door way a good long while hiccuping nervously. She giggles and starts bouncing.

"I can absorb anything and everything and nothing changes me. But you, you are chemi hysterical. Every cell of you is willing to change. You were born to expand and contract, dissolve and congeal, boil and freeze, dry and liquefy. We are as opposite as opposites can be," Emeraldine says twirling her fingers in the air like butterflies, very proud of her insight.

Euphoria motions to Emeraldine, Let's go. While the two make their way back towards the house Euphoria shares the details of her nocturnal experiments.

"I just could not stop. I had to combine the Angel Tears with my Roses. I was traveling outside of my body for hours, rolling in a sea of sparkling roses.," Euphoria's voice sounds strange, she is speaking in slow motion.

"Look at this Emeraldine, I have roses growing out of my wrist," She says, showing Emeraldine her cluster of rosebuds.

"What do you think it means?"

"I think I shall have to try that combination myself to understand better. May I please?" Emeraldine asks politely.

"Of course, they are your tears. Let's go back right now."

Back at Herbalarium again, Euphoria carefully administers the Angel Tear and Rose drop combination to Emeraldine, whose mouth is open and tongue already out eager with anticipation.

One drop and viola. The effect is instantaneous. Multi colored roses emerge all over Emeraldine's head like a flower crown.

"WOW, " Emeraldine exclaims as she clutches her head.

Euphoria is stunned.

"Look at you. Talk about chemi hysterical."

"Do you think it will it last?" Emeraldine asks.

"I have no idea. But we shall see," Euphoria grins mischievously.

Alas! Within the hour Emeraldine's roses begin drooping. By evening, all have fallen off, leaving a very disappointed Emeraldine sadly picking withered petals from her pillow case and bed sheets.

44

Euphoria's Experiments Go Wild

Next morning Euphoria comes downstairs for breakfast with a large multifaceted crystal in the center of her forehead, a gaggle of violets in full bloom on her left cheek and a tiny pine cone dangling from her right ear.

Glorious shakes his head in disbelief.

"You are something else."

"I know, I know, I got a little carried away."

Avoiding looking Glorious in the eye she goes into the hallway to get another look in the full length mirror.

"I do like the crystal though," she says, admiring the full effect of herself head to toe.

"Way too weird if you ask me. How are you going to explain this to everyone at work?"

" That is a good question. Hmmmmm....I know. I'll tie a sparkly scarf around my head and cut a hole out for the crystal to pop through. It will look artistic. Or maybe I'll just use a plain black head band. Keep it simple," she decides.

"You can tell everyone it's a Pineal Activation device," Glorious suggests.

"Now that sounds truly reasonable. Good thinking Glorious. I'm sure eventually all this will go away on its own," Euphoria says.

"I hope so, for your sake. What about these?" Glorious asks pointing to the pine cone and the violets.

"I'll just snip the violets off, put a temporary tattoo on my cheek and wear large dangly earrings, so the pine cone will blend in," Euphoria says cheerfully.

"You'd better get moving on the camouflage, so you won't be late," Glorious goes to give Euphoria a supportive hug,

"Ouch! That crystal is sharp!"

* * *

Alas, Euphoria's efforts are for naught. Later that afternoon, the violets return in full force and the pine cone sprouts a baby cone of its own. But the weirdest is thing of all is the crystal. It has shifted location slowly throughout the day finally breaking up into smaller facets in a long thin line above her eye brows.

Euphoria spends the entire evening brewing Reverse Potions in her Herbalarium. Finally, one of them work

45

Jade & Pearl Visit Helios

Helios has set into motion Manhattan Isle's first Angel Shrine. Citizens from all over town gathering to be in his presence.

The group keeps growing and expanding, transforming the atmosphere of the World Trade Center Station into a church, a temple and a mosque, all rolled into one. An inclusive, unspoken understanding and reverence for individual beliefs and traditions.

People openly sobbing, wailing, praising, chanting, singing sacred hymns in every language. Best of all are the spontaneous fits of contagious laughter. A shared unison of human joy, warmth and fellowship.

Pearl insists that Jade join her today and experience Helios for herself. When they arrive the main lobby is already over flowing with people. Many are standing or sitting on folding chairs, but most are sprawled out across the station floor on blankets.

Angel Helios's entire body is a reflecting mirror. Everyone around him can only see their own image looking at him. He communicates with each person as if they are the only one there. It is so strange and unsettling to accept at first.

Pearl and Jade squeeze in between those seated closest to Helios on the floor. As soon as Jade sits down, she hears the Angel's voice clearly inside her mind.

"I am who you choose to see," Helios says.

His voice is gentle, welcoming and strangely familiar to her.

"I choose to see you as you truly are," Jade responds.

"Close your eyes," Helios says.

Jade closes her eyes. Immediately her inner vision is filled with the vast darkness of space. Then behold, the cosmic depths reveal themselves smothered in infinite points of light.

"Ahhhhh!" Jade moans.

The vision rushes up her spine, spreading across her torso. Her whole body begins pulsating with intense pleasure.

Pearl puts her arm around Jade and whispers into her ear.

"You see what I mean," she says.

46

Euphoria Tells Pearl & Jade

Euphoria sits with Jade and Pearl in a tiny garden, out back behind The Black Needle.

"I have something I want to share with you." Euphoria says in a hushed voice, leaning in and taking a deep breath.

"I've made an amazing discovery."

Jade and Pearl pull their chairs in closer.

Euphoria tells them all about her recent experiments. She intentionally omits using the word 'Angel Tears' and substitutes it by calling it a 'Rare Crystal,' while describing her reaction to the potion in full detail.

Lifting up her hair, Euphoria reveals a luscious strawberry colored rose emerging from the right side of her neck.

Jade and Pearl gasp in unison.

"Oh my God! How is this possible?" Pearl says, totally amazed.

"May I?" Jade asks.

She leans into Euphoria's neck to inhale the rose.

"That smells Heavenly," Jade sighs.

Euphoria stifles her desire to laugh,

"If you only knew," she thinks to herself.

"What I need to know is this. Can this only happen to me? Have I stumbled upon something that can happen to other people as well? Would either of you be interested in trying it? Better even if you both are willing to try it." Euphoria asks, opening her satchel and pulling out a tiny red crystal vial.

"Just one drop. That's all I took," Euphoria says, looking each woman straight in the eye, waiting for a response.

"Did it bleed? Does it hurt?" Pearl asks.

"No. That is what was so amazing. It didn't hurt and there was no blood. Just a tingling sensation when the rose started coming up," Euphoria assures her.

Jade and Pearl look at one another. Jade jumps on it.

"I'll do it," her eyes flashing with excitement.

"How long will it take to work?" She asks.

"You should feel something right away. But the rose may take more time. It grew over night, for me." Euphoria says.

"OK, let's do it now before I change my mind," Jade says pulling her chair next to Euphoria.

Meanwhile, Pearl is looking very skeptical.

"I don't know. I'm nervous about trying it. How can you predict exactly where the rose will show up?"

"I can't. That's why I want to see how it affects someone else," Euphoria confesses.

"I'm ready," Jade says impatiently.

Euphoria smiles. Opening the vial, she squeezes the dropper very gently and places one drop on Jade's tongue.

They all hold their breath.

"OH MY GOD! I feel it. What is in this?"

Jade stands up hoping to contain the unbelievable surge of energy rushing through her body. Realizing she can't hold it, she drops to the ground rocking and rolling on the grass ecstatically. She feels something moving across her chest.

"Ooo, it's tingling me right here," she says.

Pulling down on her Tee shirt neckline to reveal the tiny spot bubbling beneath her skin. No one says a word.

They just stare and wait.

Within a few seconds a rose bud pokes its tiny head out.

Pearl and Euphoria are transfixed, as this miracle unfolds right before their very eyes.

"That was really fast," Euphoria whispers in amazement.

No one moves as the perfectly formed rose bud begins to swell, unfurling multiple layers of deep crimson velvet petals. Tendrils of fragrance wafting into the air, with such intoxicating perfume.

All three women sigh in unison.

47

Pearl & Jade After

Jade is in deep communion with her rose, a single dark red velvet flower with huge heavy petals resting on her upper left breast.

Pearl has been watching her closely for several days, observing Jade's newly found serenity and contentment since she took the potion. Finally Pearl decides she wants to experience the potion for herself. She calls Euphoria and arranges to meet her that day.

Pearl's response to the Potion is similar to Euphoria's at first. She too curls up into a ball and wails like a baby for hours. She too sleeps for 24 hours after that only she wakes up angry about everything. Screaming like a banshee at first, then switching gears and bursting into fits of uncontrollable laughter. Back and forth between these two extremes for the whole day. Finally after another night of deep sleep she wakes up calm and serene, with a stunning Lilac Rose on the lower half of her right breast.

Its fragrance is deliciously exotic and spicy. Pearl is relieved its location is easy to conceal from her patients.

What Pearl Hill cannot conceal is her new animated personality. All her former cool, subdued, introspective demeanor is gone.

There's a fiery sensual gleam in her eye and a fresh musical cadence to her voice that surprises her completely.

"Everything about being me has changed. My face has changed. My voice has changed. My thoughts have changed," Pearl tells Jade.

Jade smiles back at her with a knowing nod,

"We have been reborn," Jade declares.

"What are we now?" Pearls asks mischievously.

"Flower Children," Jade replies.

They both double over laughing hysterically and go falling on the floor, kicking their legs up into the air, clutching their ribs because it hurts so much to laugh that hard.

***

Later that evening Jade and Pearl are sitting up on the roof. The wind kicks up a slight breeze and a few drops of rain follow. It starts drizzling but they make no effort to leave.

"This feels so good," Jade says.

"Yes it does. Let's stay a while," Pearl says.

Then the rain begins to come down for real. Both women are getting completely soaked.

Suddenly Jade stands up. So then Pearl stands up.

"Are you thinking what I'm thinking?" Jade says.

"I think so. You go first," Pearl says, grinning.

Jade undresses. Pearl follows her.

"Two naked ladies *'Up On The Roof'* Pearl sings.

"Two naked ladies *'Up On The Roof'* Jades sings.

They both howl like wolves.

48

An Angel Falls Behind Faery Cakes

An Angel has landed in the back alley behind Faery Cakes. Discovered by Glorious while refreshing water bowls and cat food for local strays.

Her wings are translucent. Her skin glows like copper. She has long waves of dark amethyst hair that reach all the way down to her waist and huge sparkling violet eyes.

Having landed in such close proximity to Faery Cakes and its magical frequency, this Angel's body has not hardened to stone. Yet, she remains tethered to the concrete and visibly immobile.

Glorious is totally smashed. He names her Allure and immediately begins devising a plan to bring her inside the Cafe.

"She'd be a perfect cake stand," Grandmother Promise teases.

"Absolutely not. Better than bringing her inside, I am going to build her a rotating platform on the roof, so she can at least see the city," Glorious decides.

"I'm afraid that is not an option. Like all the other Angels she is attached to where she landed," Euphoria points out.

Glorious realizes he has conveniently forgot that detail.

"Well then, what can we turn our alleyway into?" He asks.

Promise inhales deeply and closes her eyes for a vision.

"We can create a shrine around her." she says.

Glorious eyes light up,

"That's it."

Euphoria nods enthusiastically.

"Yes! With a garden full of flowers and butterflies."

"Let me ask Allure first and see what she thinks of our idea," Glorious says and goes back outside to ask her.

"I can be whatever you choose me to be," Allure answers.

Allures voice is like a song inside Glorious's mind.

"You are my Love Supreme," he whispers back.

"I bring you into Divine Union with your self, " she says.

"You are my vision of Divine Union," Glorious purrs.

"Be aware Glorious. As you share my presence with others, it will be as powerful an experience for them, as it is for you. Many may find it difficult to leave here, once they feel it," Allure says.

Glorious contemplates the truth of what Allure has just told him. He sees the reality of her warning unfolding, as well as a plan on how to remedy it.

"I will offer access by clearly establishing the Angel Shrine's purpose. It will be regulated by a schedule of timed sessions."

Allure eyes brighten with approval,

"Yes, that will be the right way."

Glorious feels his chest swell with pride. Just the thought of taking on this additional responsibility makes his spine lengthen.

He strides back inside Faery Cakes feeling several inches taller, to tell Euphoria and Grandmother Promise his plan.

Inside the Cafe Grandmother Promise is about to read a new poem she has written for her podcast series to Euphoria.

"I am entertaining the idea of having a real Crone Salon for my listener's. Somewhere they can go all dressed up and show off and entertain one another What do you think, Euphoria?"

"And where will that take place?" Euphoria asks.

"Naturally I would need a well appointed setting, a truly Grand Salon with magnificent windows overlooking Central Park. What a shame Bella doesn't do Manhattan," Promise adds wistfully. Then she begins reading her poem aloud.

Crone Salon

Many a Spell has been woven
Many a Charm has been blessed
Many a Crone has come thru this gate
To Rest and Refresh

Chamomile tea and Lilac Creme Tarts
To comfort weary minds and soothe restless Hearts

Many a Crone sleeps in fits and starts
Then to mumble and murmur
Magical noises, Mystical nonsense

Here we try on each other's Identities and Curses
Here we solve Medicinal Crimes
We are the Experts, Doctors, Lawyers and Nurses

Crone Salon
Sets the world aright
Over Cheeses, Olives, Bread and Wine

49

Faery Cakes Angel Shrine

The Angel Shrine is underway. Glorious and his kitchen staff have scrubbed the alleyway clean and painted the walls the palest shade of robins egg blue.

There are enormous clay pots filled with Butterfly bush and Hydrangea marking off the shrine corners. Borders are lined with wild flowers and hanging baskets of cascading Indian Mint, Marjoram, Winter Savory, Creeping Thyme and Creeping Rosemary.

Natural fiber wicker chairs and love seats with moss colored cushions in a semi circle facing Allure, who is surrounded by a sea of votive candles and crystals.

Neighbors peering out their windows are visibly delighted by all the charm their alleyway is receiving.

No one has ventured forth to have an encounter with Allure as of yet. Out of respect, they await the formal opening invitation from Faery Cakes's owners.

"It appears our neighbors resonate with our vision," Glorious says in gratitude.

Yes, they are lucky in more ways than they could ever dream.

50

Emeraldine Experiments

While Euphoria has been sharing the Angel Tears with her closest friends, Jade and Pearl, Emeraldine has been doing some experimenting on her own. Actually it was more an accident that got her started.

It happened while she was gathering extra Dandelions flowers for Glorious, as his Flower Soups were getting more and more popular each day. As much as Emeraldine loves helping out and as much as she loves being in the Enchantment Garden, lately she has been feeling sad about not being able to join them down below at Faery Cakes. There still is really no way of knowing if she will turn to stone, as the other Angels have, if she leaves New Witch.

Emeraldine sighs sadly and sits down for her delicious mid day treat of fresh cucumber salad, sprouted bread, cheese and honey.

While spooning her favorite Rose Honey, her eyes well up with tears and one of her tears accidentally falls into the spoon.

Emeraldine sighs again, watching the Rose Honey soak up her tear. But then something strange and familiar happens. It begins to bubble and froth. And Presto! Inside the spoon is a sparkling pale pink crystallized Rosette, a Honey Flower!

"Oh my Goodness," Emeraldine squeals.

"Dare I eat this morsel of beauty?"

Without waiting for an answer Emeraldine pops the Rosette into her mouth. A flush of sweetness rolls on her tongue as the Rosette instantly dissolves down her throat. Her solar plexus is pulsating as a warm soothing spiral of energy begins rotating inside her belly, making her rock her back and forth.

"Ahhhhh, She moans.

"This is Heaven. Must do it again!"

Emeraldine repeats letting her tears drop into spoon fulls of honey, over and over again, producing row upon row of exquisite Honey Rosettes. Gobbling them all up as fast as she can, until she is soaring way, way up in the sky from pleasure.

Suddenly she stops herself. Realizing that she has just stumbled upon another thing her Angel Tears can do.

"I need to be still and think this through," Emeraldine says to no one in particular.

"First, I must consult the Bees before going any further. Promise is the Bee Keeper, I will ask for her help later this evening."

***

Promise is thrilled hearing about Emeraldine's discovery.

"Of course, good thinking, we must ask the Bees for their permission. We'll do that first thing tomorrow morning, when I go pour honey from their hives."

Emeraldine is ecstatic. Something incredible is about to happen, she can feel it in her bones.

"Thank you Promise. See you first thing in the morning," Emeraldine says, bouncing all the way down the hallway to her bedroom.

Prunella has been all ears to their conversation and feels Emeraldine's excitement as well. Recently she has been spending most of her nights in the grotto sleeping next to Emeraldine. She will do so again tonight, just to make certain she doesn't miss a thing tomorrow morning.

" I wonder what those Honey Rosettes will do to me?" she asks, her eye lids growing heavy with dreaming.

51

Emeraldine & The Star Bees

Next morning Promise and Emeraldine visit the Bee Hives. There are eight of them in a semi circle at the garden's edge. Promise clears her throat and asks loudly,

"Would any hive here like to participate in Emeraldine's Angel Tear and Honey experiment?"

Among the hives the first one to respond to Promise's question is Hive No. 5. A burst of pollen flies into the air and several worker Bees zoom out.

"We Do!" They say, buzzing loudly.

"Excellent," Promise exclaims.

"Emeraldine, please explain what happened yesterday," Promise suggests as she goes about pouring honey from the rest of the hives.

Emeraldine opens her hand and shows the worker Bees one of her Angel Tear & Honey Rosettes.

"This is what happened when one of my tears fell into a spoonful of your Rose Honey yesterday," she says.

The worker Bees gather around the Honey Rosette in her hand. They sit on it and begin nibbling away. By the sound of their buzzing Emeraldine can hear that they are getting very excited.

They begin bouncing up and down on the Honey Rosette like children on a trampoline, their voices getting higher and higher.

Suddenly more droning Bees come out of Hive No. 5. Before Emeraldine can stop them, the Bees lift the Honey Rosette out of her hand gently into the air and carry it back into their Hive. One of the Bees buzzes into Emeraldine's ear, to tell her they are bringing her Honey Rosette to their Queen.

Hive No.5 is buzzing louder than ever. It is obvious the Honey Rosette is at the center of all the commotion. This gets Emeraldine so excited, her wings start flapping wildly.

After a few minutes a line of Drone Bees emerge bearing a message from their Queen. Her Royal Highness requests Emeraldine come closer and share her Angel Tears directly into the Hive.

Emeraldine, deeply moved by the Queen's invitation, that her eyes begin glistening at once. She goes to Hive No.5 and hovers directly over the opening and begins weeping for joy.

The effect is more startling than anyone could have imagined. The entire Hive transforms into a sparking translucent prism. Every detail of its inner workings are now visible from the outside. From its Bees Wax cones sheltering Baby Bees, to its Propolis lined cells, to the Queen's Palace and her Guardians.

The Queen herself undergoes transformation. Her body begins oscillating bands of light from deep indigo to the palest of violet. Her Eggs look like tiny diamonds and are changing into sparkling diamond like Larvae as well. By evening all of the Larvae transformed into Pupae are shimmering Baby Crystal Bees.

The buzzing continues all day and all night long, at a pitch so high, it is beyond human hearing capacity. The intensity of its frequency causes the rest of the other Hives an overload of excitation and a long sleepless night in anticipation of what is to come.

Next morning Hive No. 5 is a totally saturated cone of brilliant light. All worker Bees and Drones are beyond dazzling to behold. The Queen Bee is a magnificent shimmering rainbow of Light.

Emeraldine and Promise are equally stunned at what has transpired in the last twenty-four hours. The other seven Bee Hives are unusually quiet. Mesmerized by Hive No. 5's transformation, they hold their breath.

Promise goes to Hive No. 5 and removes the top box to begin gathering the honey she expects to find there. Quickly putting on her sun glasses as the light within is too intensely bright to look at.

She begins pouring that first frame of honey into her bucket almost swooning over the scent of its shimmering gold ambrosia. It is intoxicating! This honey is like nothing like she has ever experienced before.

"What will you call this honey, Emeraldine?" Promise asks respectfully.

"Angel Honey," Emeraldine murmurs softly.

"Star Bee Honey," buzz Hive No. 5 Bees in unison.

Meanwhile, Emeraldine has been telepathically conversing with the Queen Bee, asking her for more details of her transformation, as well as those of her Hive's.

"Is it permanent?" She asks the Queen.

"Yes, I believe your Angel Tears have upgraded our DNA. We are so much more now than we have ever been before, even more magical than we were as New Witch Bees. We have become Star Bees, Members of the Galactic Bee Federation of the Multiverse," Queen Bee tells her.

Emeraldine's eyes start spinning a Circles of Stars, just from hearing this information.

"Oh My dear. I believe your DNA has been upgraded as well from eating our Star Bee Honey," Queen Bee observes.

Emeraldine blushes strawberry pink and giggles,
"I know. Isn't it grand?"
"Star Bee Angel Honey," Promise winks at Emeraldine.
"Looks like we now have a new line of Honey for Faery Cakes Bakery Cafe this summer," she adds.
"I can't wait to share the news with Euphoria and Glorious," Emeraldine says proudly.

Meanwhile Bella, who has naturally been listening in on all the events of this morning, has begun making plans of her own.

"Now where be the best location inside me for a Star Bee Angel Honey office?" She asks herself.

52

Jade & Pearl In Conference With Euphoria

Euphoria is in Riverside Park with Jade and Pearl, listening to them describe their experiences since taking the Rose Potion.

They both are wearing vintage styled white eyelet ruffled blouses and long flowery print skirts from the '60's. Most definitely not typical of their former fashion sensibility, Euphoria observes.

"We are changing daily. We see the difference in each other's eyes. We hear it in each other's voices" Pearl says.

"We spent the whole night on the roof in the rain, completely soaked and we did not leave," Jade adds.

"And look at this," Pearl says, pulling her blouse up to show Euphoria her new rose.

"This morning we each have a new rose growing exactly where our old ones fell off in the rain," Jade says, pulling her blouse down to reveal her new rose.

"What is in this potion Euphoria?" Jade probes.

"You haven't told us everything, have you?" Pearl asks. Euphoria's stomach tightens as she puts her guard up.

"You'll have to trust me on this. I cannot reveal my source just yet. I wish I could, but I can't right now. And even if you knew, it wouldn't change anything. Everything would still be happening exactly the way it is and the consequences would still be unknown.

All I can tell you is that I have never done this before. No one, as far as I know, has ever done this before. We are on the cusp of something really big. We're going through it together," Euphoria emphasizes with utmost seriousness.

"So? What exactly are we becoming?" Pearl asks, looking deep into Euphoria's eyes.

"You tell me," Euphoria says and mirrors her depth back.

"I feel like I am morphing into a rose. How else could I have sat in the rain all night long like that and feel perfectly fine about it?" Pearl says.

"And another thing, my eyesight has literally improved over night. I don't need my readers anymore," Pearl adds.

Euphoria decides it is time to ask Pearl about the possibility of trying the potion on one of her patients.

"Pearl, is there anyone coming to your clinic for regular weekly treatments?" she probes.

"Yes, a few do," Pearl can feel the direction Euphoria is going in.

"Would you be open to introducing any of them to the Potion?" Euphoria asks her eyes twinkling mischievously.

"Actually I was thinking the same thing. There is someone I think would try it," Pearl grins at the telepathic moment.

"Good, ask him. Explain that it is organic plant medicine, cutting edge for sure, with amazing benefits, " Euphoria says.

Pearl smiles to herself, " now how did she know it was a he? "

"He'll be in tomorrow. I'll let you know what he says," Pearl says laughing.

"Great. Here's an extra vial, just for him," Euphoria says and hands her a small wooden box.

"We are on the brink of something huge. I can feel it inside every cell of my body," Jade says beaming.

For a moment there, Euphoria thinks she sees a Circle of Star Eyes spinning inside Jades gold eyes and lets out a tiny gasp.

The three of them link hands. Squeezing tight, they raise up their arms and let out a long wolf howl.

53

A Green Drink

Glorious is perusing the health food section at his local supermarket. Smiling at the bottles labeled Green Drink.

In New Witch, a Green Drink means absorbing with the entire landscape through one's senses. Witchess can taste color. They can inhale minerals and herbal essence through the soles of their feet.

Green Drink Recipe
In a blender add:
1 cup of Spring Water
Puree: 1 inch Peeled Fresh Ginger
1 Tsp. Fresh Lemon Juice
2-3 Stalks of Celery
1 Peeled Cucumber
Add Fresh Arugula, Spinach, Bok Choy or Kale
Add Fresh Dandelion, Parsley, Cilantro, Basil, Thyme
Slice of Onion, Crushed Garlic, Pink Salt
Splash of Apple Cider Vinegar
Splash of Aloe Juice
1 Tbsp. of Kimchi, Sauerkraut and or pinch of Horse Radish

54

Glorious & The Angel Tears

Glorious is sitting beneath Witch Hazel's tree writing a new take out menu for Faery Cakes Bakery Cafe

Faery Cakes Flower Soups In A Box
Just add hot water and watch your bowl blossom...
Flowers pods unfurl their tender leaves and buds
Herbs and Spices swirl in fragrant tasty spirals
Nuts and seeds popping crunchy morsels of delight

Flavor and Savor Mushroom, Bean, Fruit & Nut Pies
Mushroom Pies mighty and meaty, steeped in savory marinades
Black Bean Pies baked to perfection, will melt in your mouth
Cool Green Fruit & Nut Pies, filled with Blue Green Algae
Cashew or Pistachio Custard
Topped with Raspberries, Blueberries or Blackberries

*Stay Tuned for my upcoming cook book
The Orgasmic Palette by Glorious Green

Euphoria has been looking for Glorious. She senses this might be the right time and describes the effect of taking the Angel Tears to him and challenges him to try it.

"All you'll need is one drop," she says.

"One drop?"

"Yes, one drop and then wait to see what happens," Euphoria advises. Glorious opens his mouth sticking his tongue out like a child about to laugh. Euphoria places a single drop of the Angel Tears on his tongue and watches him as he swallows the drop and has the same response she had.

"Feels like a mouthful, right?"

"Whoa," he gasps,

"What was that?"

His Sapphire eyes immediately cloud over. His lips begin quivering. He wraps his arms around his body and curls up into a ball on the grass and starts wailing like a new born baby.

Euphoria knows he will want to go through this alone. His journey will be deep, just like hers was. She leaves him there and heads back to the house.

Glorious weeps for hours on end. By evening he is so totally rung out he cannot stand up. Instead he crawls into Witch Hazel's house and sleeps like a stone.

Waking at dawn, all Glorious can think about is Emeraldine. Before leaving for work he finds her, takes her in his arms and kisses her passionately. He doesn't let go, even when she screams,

"Ouch, that burns."

Emeraldine swoons and has to be given smelling salts. The rest of the day she is seen floating around New Witch in a daze.

Later that evening, she confides to Bella,

"Who knew? If you happen to be an Angel and you give your Tears to your unrequited love, it acts as a Love Potion."

55

Crimson Witch Meets Her Angel

Euphoria's cousin, Crimson Witch runs The Red Shoes Dance Studio on the corner of Broadway and Greene Street, right across the street from where Grandmother Promise host her podcast series.

It is also where Crimson Witch rehearses her astonishing troupe of Sky Dancers.

After teaching her last class of the day, Crimson goes to clean out the dressing room. That is when she notices two bare feet behind one of the curtained stalls.

"Sorry, I didn't know anyone was still here," she says.

Waiting for a reply and getting none, she calls out again,

"Are you OK?"

Still no response.

Crimson goes over to the dressing stall and peeks behind the long red silk curtain.

"Ahhhh." she screams.

There within the dressing stall stands a magnificent towering Angel. Alabaster skin. Raven black, iridescent wings. Jet black hair, pulled tight into a mound on the crown of her head. She is wearing a long black tunic, with her arms crossed in front of her chest, as if protecting herself.

Her elongated oval face chiseled with features identical to that of the legendary mother of modern dance, dancer / choreographer, Martha Graham.

Dumbfounded, Crimson Witch remains speechless.

"I am who you choose to see," The Angel says, into Crimson's mind with a distinctly dramatic, crisply enunciated voice.

"Martha Graham?" Crimson asks, overwhelmed with emotion.

"For you, yes, Martha Graham," The Angel replies.

56

Emeraldine Explores Bella

Emeraldine has been exploring Bella and Bella is absolutely thrilled to have someone to show off her secret chambers to.

After midnight Bella lights a candle and leads Emeraldine down a new corridor. The air here smells slightly perfumed and dry. At the end of the hallway are two enormous gilded gold doors. Bella dramatically flings them open to reveal her most treasured secret. An eighteenth century Palace Ballroom.

Emeraldine is beside herself, squealing with joy as she enters its opulent splendor. The ballroom floor is a shimmering lake made of polished Opal. High above are three enormous crystal chandeliers suspended in thin air. A balcony tier gracefully curving around the entire ballroom, is just begging for an audience to fill its powder blue velvet chairs.

Emeraldine rushes on to the ball room floor, gliding as if on ice. From somewhere hidden, an orchestra begins to play. It is a waltz. She whirls round and round imagining she dancing with Glorious.

Then the chandeliers grow dim and suddenly the entire ballroom is filled with fire flies swirling around Emeraldine, who is just about ready to swoon from the beauty of it all.

"Oh Bella, what am I to do? Love burns. Love's flame is too painful for me," Emeraldine confesses.

Bella sends a warm breeze through the ballroom, letting Emeraldine know she hears her heart.

"Bella! You are such a tender house," Emeraldine says dropping to her knees, she kisses the ballroom floor.

The orchestra starts up again this time accompanied by a rich mezzo soprano's voice, singing, *"I Could Have Danced All Night."*

"Bella! Is that you?" Emeraldine asks, pretending she's surprised.

Another breeze gently ushers Emeraldine out of the Ballroom, down another passage way to an intricately carved wooden door.

This one opens to a long gallery overflowing with tapestries, fabrics and strange objects. Like a museum with multiple panoramas from varying time periods. The History of New Witch told in "Scissors and Buttons, Lace and Leather, Bone and Feathers."

Bella shows Emeraldine the Sewing Room, where she keeps the treasures from the ancestor's arrival in New Witch. They brought with them all their Lenape life skills and traditions. They made their own clothes from deer skin, lined them with fur of rabbit and fox. They made buttons from bones, wove baskets from Sweet Grass, strung necklaces with beads made from seeds and shells.

Bella shows Emeraldine her ingenious 'hands on' approach to handling the objects she treasures. After discovering a brass door knocker shaped as a pair of hands, Bella has employed them exclusively to turn keys, open the locks of boxes, trunks and wardrobe closets. Her greatest joy is using them to turn pages of books she loves to read while peering through a pair of floating spectacles.

Using them now she pulls a book out of one of the trunks and sends it floating between the brass hands over to Emeraldine.

The book's cover is made of wood and its pages made of deer skin. There are mysterious, wonderfully drawn symbols inside and between the pages are translations written on parchment made of cotton. Emeraldine recognizes Euphoria's handwriting.

Fascinated, Emeraldine begins to read out loud.

"Our ancestors prayers were the first songs sung in New Witch. They were songs of gratitude for all they had been given. This forest sanctuary far from the turmoil below. Songs of thanksgiving for the abundance they received, for the crops they planted and harvested. These songs have been passed down from generation to generation.

Our Great Grandfather, Maestro Orlean composed music to accompany them, while preserving the essence embedded in their original tongue. We will always honor the Lenape language and spirit here in New Witch.

Somewhere inside our house, Bella keeps Maestro Orlean's studio. His Bosendorfer Grand piano is still there, as well as his writing desk and filing cabinets over flowing with his musical compositions.

He taught Grandmother Promise to play on that piano when she was a young girl. He taught her our ancestor's songs as well as all the best classical composers.

When I was a very little girl, I remember Grandmother Promise asking for Bella to open Maestro Orlean's studio. I still remember her playing the Bosendorfer. Her hands flying over its silken ivory and ebony keys. The fiery music and her memories igniting her fingers, they danced violently upon the keys that day.

I have asked her to play the piano again, but she says her heart isn't in it anymore. She hasn't played in over sixty years, not since the death of her daughter, my mother, Peace Green."

57

Angel Tears Potion

Grandmother Promise and Euphoria are in the Enchantment Garden gathering Sweet Annie for Star Bee Honey infusion.

"How do you explain the effects of your Angel Potion?"

"I am not absolutely sure. All I know is that it can alter human consciousness. Look at Jade and Pearl. Literally overnight. It's as if the Tears merge with the life force of Terra Rose and go straight into our DNA," Euphoria says.

Promise has been aware that Euphoria has undergone some significant changes as well since taking the Potion, but has resisted asking about it, until now.

"What about you? Notice anything different in yourself?" she probes gently.

Euphoria smiles knowingly.

"Yes I have and thank you for noticing. I am softer, lighter, less controlling. What say you? What else have you noticed about me?"

Euphoria looks deeply into her Grandmother's sea green eyes.

"Yes, I see that you are all those, but I'm not getting a clear picture of what it means just yet, Promise says, somewhat vaguely.

"I was thinking, you should call your potion Bee A Rose," Promise says on a lighter note.

"Bee A Rose, I love it," Euphoria clasps her hands together just like Emeraldine always does.

"If this potion is more than a botanical decoration. If in fact, it actually alters human consciousness, as you have implied it does. If it permanently alters our DNA, do you realize what this could mean?"

Promise widens her eyes,

"Doctor Euphoria Frankenschtein," Promise says laughing.

Euphoria plays along with her Grandmother and makes her eyes deliberately Spin Stars like a tornado.

"Das is true!!"

58

Daemon Cortez

Pearl has one of her favorite patients on the table this morning. Daemon Cortez, who also happens to be Jades youngest brother. Daemon is one of those rare human beings born with both female and male genitalia and is known as a Hermaphrodite.

That alone has been the root of so much stress in his life.

Pearl has been treating Daemon since he reached puberty, six years ago. He is now nineteen and a freshman at Manhattan School of Music. In spite of all the progressive social attitudes around gender these days, coming out as a Hermaphrodite is traumatic.

Pearl perceives Daemon as dominantly male. He has broad, muscular shoulders, a thick neck and a strong jaw line in sharp contrast to his long, slender arms, legs and delicate hands and feet. Most of all its in his eyes. They are mercurial, sometimes green, sometimes gold, sometimes chestnut, and they always have that hungry look. That ready to pounce on you look.

Having bleached his jet black hair, platinum blond and being six feet two inches tall makes him stand out in any crowd.

"I may think like a man, but I feel like a woman," Daemon tells Pearl, as she takes his pulse reading.

"The women I attract are disappointed when they discover my deepest desire is to be ravaged by them. They want to be ravished by me, not the other way around. Then the gay men I go out with end up resenting me for being too much like a real women. Especially my not wanting to be their freaky sex toy." Daemon says in despair, "How could God create this? I'm a mess."

Daemon's shame and self loathing show up regularly in his acupuncture sessions. Pearl begins to say something then changes her mind. Instead, she places several needles along Daemon's scalp to calm him down. Then she applies more needles along his liver and gall bladder meridians, to unblock the stagnant chi energy being held in there. Daemon's anger has been stored and repressed along those channels his entire life. Finally she responds.

"I think you have been given an extraordinary opportunity in this life. You get to experience both male and female instincts. You get to explore the most primal needs and desires from each genders perspective," she explains.

"But who will want me?" Daemon's lips are quivering, as he stifles his tears.

"Your question should be, who do I want?" Pearl says adding three more needles around Daemon's belly button.

"Who do I want?" Daemon repeats.

"Yes. That person already exists. Invite them into your life. Ask from the place of already knowing they are here." Pearl adds smiling, pointing to Daemon's heart.

She lights up a moxie stick and holds the smoking herb over each needle. As the scent of Mugwort fills the treatment room, Daemon sighs, he loves steeping in its rich earthy fragrance.

Daemon slips into a reverie inspired by Pearl's question.

"I'm gonna let you bake a while,"she says, leaving the room.

"Who do I want?" Daemon repeats.

An image floats into his mind's eye. He sees a dark skin female warrior, with male genitals.

"One of my own kind," Daemons says to himself.

"My soulmate is a woman like me, who loves me and loves how we are both male and female."

For the first time in his life Daemon understands that there must be others in the world, just like him and that he can and will find them.

After Daemon's treatment, Pearl suggests they sit outside in the little garden behind the clinic.

"Your sister and I have recently been introduced to a very special herbal elixir made by our friend Euphoria Green. I believe you know her as well."

"Of course! I eat at Faery Cakes almost everyday," Daemon says.

"We both think you would benefit by taking it as well," Pearl says, lowering her voice to almost a whisper.

"But there is one thing. You must promise to refrain from telling anyone about it, not even your closest friends or family."

"Am I going to turn into a frog?" Daemon giggles nervously.

"I want to let you experience it for yourself, before I tell you any more. I can assure you it is totally organic and safe," Pearl says, taking the Potion vial out of her pocket.

Daemon takes one look at the shimmering red crystal vial and nods his head emphatically 'Yes'.

"Okay. I am going place one single drop on your tongue. It works very fast, so we'll just sit here and see what happens.

Daemon sticks his tongue out. His eyes are dancing with excitement for this new adventure.

The effect of the Potion surprises both of them. Daemon immediately falls into a trance. A spectacular vision unfolds, like a film streaming from his third eye. Daemon sees crowds of people walking along the streets of New York City. They are moving very slowly. Their bodies are translucent and are filled with soil. There are roots and stems growing on the inside. Flowers blossoming outside their bodies. Their eyes are sparkling like gem stones.

As the vision dissolves Daemon filled with incredible sense of well being and joy. He jumps up and shouts

"Thank You Pearl," he says, while hugging her tightly.

Daemon takes off running. A song is being born. Its melody and words, rushing like a river sweeping him up into the air. He is soaring upon its wings all the way back uptown to his apartment.

SONG
" I Am Magic "

I Am Magic
And a million little Sparklings, begin bubbling in my blood stream
I Am Magic
And a billion little Sparklings, begin dancing in my bones and under my skin
Watch me open, Like a flower
Every cell inside me tells me I'm connected, to it all
I Am Magic
And a trillion little Sparklings, begin pulsing through my finger tips
I Am Magic
And a zillion little Sparklings, begin singing on my tongue
and on my lips
Watch me open, Like a flower
Every cell explodes, beyond my body grows, connections to it all
Watch me spiral, down to my core
There's a world beneath my feet, showing me everywhere is home
I Am Magic

The following day Daemon notices a tiny pale lilac colored rose bud on his wrist. It smells so heavenly and re activates yesterday's vision. He calls Pearl right away and asks her if it is possible for Euphoria to use lilacs.

"I absolutely adore lilacs. Is that possible? Can she use lilacs in place of the roses?"

Euphoria is delighted by Daemon's reaction and offers to test using lilacs on herself first and let him know. A simple variation using her best lilac tincture. The result is tiny lilac clusters delicately blooming under her skin, so pale in color they are barely visible on her arms.

"They are stunning," she tells Pearl the following morning and hands her a vial of Lilac Potion for Daemon.

Daemon's reaction to the Lilac Potion is quite dramatic. Every inch of his body looks as if lilacs are silk screened into his flesh. Full lilac cones sprout on his chest and usher in wave after wave of orgasmic pleasure, leaving Daemon panting with satisfaction.

"I am a totally freaking awesome freak now, " Daemon curls into a ball hysterically laughing.

***

"Like I wasn't freaky enough before, right?" He says to Pearl and Jade over dinner at their loft.

"The strangest thing is that I actually feel like I am a lilac. My whole body oozes its fragrance. Bees and butterflies are rushing over to me in Riverside park. I go to sit there on the grass at night and I feel like I am a lilac bush, and no one bothers me. It's like they don't even see me sitting there and all I can think about is rain. I can't wait for it to start raining so I can drink, drink, drink,"

Daemon hiccups, as if he is drunk.

In a way he is drunk. Drunk the way a lilac in full bloom swells up completely fulfilled and content with her beauty, her scent, her magic. For the first time in Daemon's life, he feels exalted and wholly him/her self.

Later that evening Daemon writes in his journal...

> *My fellow musician's,*
> *Grieve not*
> *The lack of Google plays,*
> *Downloads, or Streaming hits,*
> *Embrace the truth,*
> *The Value of your Skill and Devotion*
> *Is wholly found in the Joy of the Doing*
> *There, in Tone, in Melody, in Rhythm*
> *Your Joy Travels*
> *Into the Vast Ethereal Depths of Space*
> *Amplified in Galactic Arenas*
> *Your Songs Live On in Eternity*
> *Unlimited Frequencies throughout the Multiverse*
> *Music is Food in Inter Stellar Realms*
> *While you Sing and Play your Instruments Here on Earth,*
> *Your Doing, Is the Gold, Is the Diamond,*
> *The Act itself, Is Your Abundance*
> *Your Creation Is Your Divine Essence*
> *Be The I Am Music!*

59

Witch Hazel The Dryad's Story

Euphoria and Emeraldine are sitting in the Herbalarium looking through some of Witch Hazel's books on Plant Medicine.

"Witch Hazel was already here when our ancestors first arrived. Talking to a tree spirit was not strange to them. The Lenape had always conversed with Nature Spirits on Manhattan Isle.

Witch Hazel helped them build their first house, dig their first well and plant their first garden. She taught them how to use the magic of New Witch and has been an essential member of our family for generations. I can read you some of her autobiography, if you like," Euphoria offers.

"Yes, please," Emeraldine replies.

She follows Euphoria over to her desk where she pulls out a very unusual looking book out of one of the drawers. Its cover is made from the bark of Witch Hazel's tree. There are three copper clasps with gold bindings. A face has been carved on the front cover.

Emeraldine smiles as the face begins to move, protruding and receding like an ocean wave. It is the face of a very much younger Witch Hazel.

Euphoria begins reading aloud.

"How I Came To Be A Tree"
by Witch Hazel

"No one is born a tree, unless one is a seed from a tree to begin with. So my birth came as great surprise to my mother and my father.

How was she, my mother, able to explain this grotesque emanation from her womb to the world?

I emerged as a horribly shriveled creature, with multiple shades of brown and gray skin. I had gold eyes and black hair. And while all my limbs were perfectly formed, there were strange fringes of long dark roots dangling from the inner sides of my arms and legs and from either side of my rib cage. The midwife let out a scream. My father and my mother fainted. I was a monster. Too horrific to behold.

Devastated, my parents decided to get rid of me. They took me as far away from their home as possible by foot, deep into the forest and buried me near a stream where the earth was moist and easy enough to dig deep. They left no stone, nor marker, nothing to show this was my grave.

I was buried alive. Eyes wide open. I inhaled. My lungs expanded. I swallowed the earth as if it were mother's milk and sank peacefully into her arms. My roots purred with delight. Snails and insects of all sorts entertained me. I could hear the frogs singing and owls hooting and the wolves howling at night above me. I was safe. I was loved. Nourished by earth, rain and sun."

Euphoria stops reading. Looking at Emeraldine she sees how heart wrenching Witch Hazel's story is for her to hear. Closing the book, she points out positive results of such a difficult beginning.

"Witch Hazel's life is abundant in ways we cannot begin to imagine. She is brilliant. A true sage. Her books are the foundation for all the Herbal Wisdom classes I teach at Faery Cakes.

Her insight into the plant kingdom is profound. Listen to these. Here are some of my favorite Witch Hazel quotes,"

QUOTES by WITCH HAZEL

*"Treat herbs like strangers.
Make introductions, then social calls.
Get to know each other before diving into bed with them."*

"To step outside is to step within."

*"Nature is not a backdrop to our existence.
Nature is the vessel from which we are poured into being."*

"Communion is my first language."

"Where can I go to be more myself than here?"

*"Impatience and boredom are unreal. They are distractions,
a postponement of utter joy and revelation."*

"Nature is not a landscape. Nature is an interior presence so vast, so finely nuanced, overflowing with the giving of God."

"Tune in, the Green is talking."

"There is listening to be discovered. Listen, and Just be !"

Euphoria pauses, then reaches for Witch Hazel's newest yet to be published book entitled *The Witchess of New Witch, New York*.

"The Witchess of New Witch, New York merge with Nature through all their senses. Here in New Witch we say, 'I am under the Spell of Violet or Carrot or Pepper or Cinnamon.' That is how we express our communion with the soul of each plant and their hold upon us.

Witchess experience food as a sacrament. To ingest food one does not love is blasphemous. Having a sincere relationship with what we eat, is of utmost importance. For instance, a peach that does not want to be eaten, should be left alone. It is a sin to do otherwise."

Saturated with new insights from listening to Euphoria share Witch Hazel's wisdom, Emeraldine asks,

"May I borrow this book for a while?"

The face on the cover of Witch Hazel's autobiography has been listening to their conversation and smiles.

"Of course you may. This is the perfect book for you to be reading at the moment." Euphoria says, placing the book gently into Emeraldine's eager hands.

60

Rock Soup

Euphoria is on a roll....
"There are ancestral recipes we hold back offering to our friends below, as it only provokes questions and curiosity we seek to avoid.

Rock Soup for instance, one of our most treasured family recipes, was created by Witch Hazel to feed our ancestors when they first arrived. She is responsible for naming them the WeKansas, which means The Greens in Lenape.

It was autumn 1642, the beginning of their first year in New Witch, before Bella the House existed. They had built a small stone lodge, just like the one they had lived in on Manhattan Isle.

The first thing they cooked over the fire were the stones they had gathered. They called these stones 'Singing Stones.'

They were the precious gems embedded inside the layers of large rocks next along the river and lying in smaller stream beds in New Witch forest. They glistened in the sun and glowed in the moonlight. Our ancestors had the ability to hear the stones frequencies in ways we do not understand but hope to once again."

"There were Emeralds as big as walnuts, Rubies the size of plums, Sapphires the size of robin's eggs and Diamonds as large as chestnuts. As well as other gemstones such as Opals, Topaz, Tourmaline, Citrine, Aquamarine, Garnets, Amethysts and Onyx.

Our ancestors made huge clay pots from the river's mud and simmered the Singing Stones in them over the fire. It was Holy Spirit that entered the Singing Stones and infused them with miraculous powers. One or two sips of Rock Soup could sustain them in perfect health through out the winter. Sprinkling a few drops of Rock Soup upon the ground and Three Sisters; Corn, Bean and Squash would bloom right through the snow and ice.

They sang and danced in gratitude for the gifts Great Mystery had given them. Gifts that would allow them to thrive for generations to come. The WeKansas never went hungry. The older animals of the forest knew when their own lives were coming to an end. They would lie down near the lodge; deer and bear, rabbit and fox, and offer their meat and the warmth of their skins to the family within. Mutual tears of respect and humility flowed. The eternal dance of Life. One Breath, One Body, One Spirit."

Euphoria takes a deep breath and goes quiet, letting the silence say what words cannot.

61

Euphoria Confesses

Euphoria finally confesses her feelings for Adore to Emeraldine. Realizing that Euphoria could use some guidance on how things work with Angels, Emeraldine offers to explain.

"Angels do not think the way humans do. The longer I remain in New Witch, the more I have come to understand what it means to have choices. Human beings have choices. They can choose their thoughts and desires. Angels have no Self to do that with. Our only Self is to serve the needs and desires of others. We desire nothing for ourselves. Our only real desire is that we accomplish the task asked of us. If we were to have our own needs and desires, we'd never be capable of fulfilling all that is asked of us.

As I see it, Adore is not guilty for not choosing you, as you seem to think. He is simply not equipped to choose you. It is you who must decide how he can serve you," she says.

Euphoria's eyes light up with the dawn of recognition.

"Oh dear. This is such a huge revelation. Now what do I do?"

"Go back to Adore and tell him now you understand,"

"OK, that I can do. Oh Emeraldine, I love you," Euphoria says, taking Emeraldine's face into her hands, kissing both her cheeks.

Giggling, Emeraldine blushes and squeals,
"I feel that all over," she says.
A Circle of Stars begins spinning inside her eyes.
Euphoria gasps,
"I don't believe it. You?"
"Me?
Emeraldine grins wildly.
"I am Witchessssss!!! she squeals with unabashed delight.

62

Euphoria Returns To Adore Again

Euphoria is so excited about seeing Adore again she is trembling inside and out. Holding her breath, she circles in a loop around Lady Liberty several times before she finally gathers enough courage to get any closer. She hovers in the air a few feet away from him.

"Is it just my imagination? Or does he really look different." she thinks to herself.

Adore senses her presence.

Euphoria moves closer to him. She positions herself on his right, looks straight ahead and closes her eyes as she begins to speak.

"I want to apologize for the way I ran off last time," she says.

Adore is quiet at first. Then he says softly,

"You understand now."

"Yes. I do. I am to do the choosing, So, here is what I choose."

Euphoria opens her eyes and glides in closer facing him.

"I choose you to choose me," She says.

She so likes hearing herself say those words, she says them again. Adore's eyes begin to glisten. Something stirs in his chest.

Emboldened, Euphoria continues,

"I choose you to want me. I choose you to need me. I choose you to cherish me. I choose you to please me. I choose you to feel me. I choose you to breathe with me. I choose you to walk with me and talk with me and be with me and hold me and sleep with me."

This unabashed declaration makes Euphoria light headed and giddy. She starts to laugh uncontrollably. Grabbing a hold of her knees she begins rolling like a ball in mid air.

Adores eyes have turned into pools of midnight blue with dancing stars. His body glows. His wings shooting sparks of gold high into the air. He is ecstatic.

Waves of pleasure begin oscillating between the two of them. Euphoria absorbs his ecstatic response. She rides his energy like riding a horse, her body undulating in wild abandon.

"Here we are, between Heaven and Earth. We cut to the chase, we do not waste words. Love Asks. Love is Given," Adore says.

After their orgasmic communion, Euphoria flings her body over Adore. Draping herself around him as far as she can reach, she remains glued to him till morning.

63

Euphoria Next Morning

This morning's Sigil flight is unlike any other flight ever taken. Euphoria is singing the body electric, zipping through the air, diving like a roller coaster between towers and sky scrapers. Her joy fanning out in waves of triumphant, ecstatic frequencies all over Manhattan Isle.

Spring time is busy bee time, as more people head uptown to sample and savor the magic of Faery Cakes Bakery Cafe. A line of customers has been forming outside since 8:00 am.

Euphoria arrives with her eyes spinning Stars furiously under violet tinted sun glasses. Merrily she goes about filling the bakery display counter with Strawberry, Orange, Lemon and Lavender cupcakes smothered in Violets and Pansies. Next, she fills porcelain tea cups with Rose Cacao Pudding, topped with crushed gem stones, then slices samples of freshly baked fruit and nut bread, cardamon spice cranberry scones and pistachio mint cookies.

All the human voices in the Cafe sound like hummingbirds. Every order placed, is a Divine request, to be fulfilled as an act of Grace. The day whirls by like a waltz. Euphoria has to stop herself several times from levitating in the Cafe.

Back home in New Witch later that afternoon, Euphoria heaps a pile of thank yous upon Emeraldine for her advice.

"Emeraldine, I cannot thank you enough. You were so right. When I told Adore all the things I choose him to be for me, it set off the most ecstatic, transcendent ethereal union between us."

Emeraldine applauds Euphoria's success.

"I should follow my own advice and reveal my whole heart to your brother Glorious," she says and begins weeping.

"Why are you crying?" Euphoria asks.

"I have another confession to make. My Tears have bewitched Glorious. That is the only reason he desires me."

"Oh my goodness! Emeraldine, nothing could be further from the truth. Your Angel Tears liberate our deepest emotions. They reveal only that which we truly desire. And for your information, Witchess cannot be bewitched. We are immune to such things. Curses, hexes, spells can not and do not cross our threshold. We are irrevocably sovereign beings," Euphoria says reassuringly.

"Euphoria, you're words so do resonate the truth in my heart. I now and forever, liberate myself from all illusions of self doubt!" Emeraldine says, levitating a few inches up off the floor.

"Whoa!!! Did you see that?" She says.

64

Euphoria Dreams Of Adore

Every night New Witch, New York curls up her edges and tucks herself in. Nocturnal creepers and peepers take turn ruling the forest. The scent of Night Blooming Jasmine goes sweeping over the Enchantment Garden's pan flora with a lullaby of fragrance.

Emeraldine has taken to sleeping next to the Bee Hives, so Bella has created a bed for her there made entirely of clouds.

Cloud pillows, cloud sheets, cloud blankets that surprisingly keep her warm and dry, contrary to clouds being moist. Bella's magic is potent.

Meanwhile Glorious is sprawled out inside his bedroom on a massive four poster bed, built by great-great-great Grandfather Onkuntewakan.

Grandmother Promise is happily snoring away in her own bed, on azure silk sheets, under a cozy hand made quilt, surrounded by silk pillows tucked just right, to keep her joints and muscles in proper alignment through the night.

In the other wing of the house, Prunella the Cat is hiding behind a Victorian steamer trunk in Euphoria's bedroom, convinced mouse will soon make an appearance.

Since Euphoria's most recent encounter with Adore, she has taken to eating shortbread cookies in bed at night, leaving moist crumbs scattered about the floor. Surely mouse cannot resist.

* * *

Euphoria is asleep and dreaming of Adore. He is huge as a Pterodactyl and she is riding upon his back. They are flying at an incredible speed. His wings act like a magnets, pulling vast amounts of ashen gray particles out of the planet's core. The particles pass through Adores body and undergo purification. They transform into magnificent multi colored Mycelium spores and go falling like rain back to Earth.

Suddenly Euphoria is aware of a loud purring sound. She opens her eyes to see Prunella is stretched across her chest.

"You were twitching something fierce in your sleep. So I thought I'd better climb on board to see where you were going," Prunella whispers.

"Where was I?" Euphoria asks, yawning and stretching.

"I don't know exactly. You were flying very high on the back of a bird man, vacuuming dead things up from the ground. Then I got distracted." Prunella opens her front paws and shows Euphoria two baby mice, one curled up in each paw sleeping.

"Where did you get them?" Euphoria asks, concerned.

"I found them in your dream. So, I guess they belong to you, that is if you want them," Prunella adds with a sly grin.

The look on Euphoria's face tells all.

"OK. I'll go put them in the garden," Prunella says, resigned.

Euphoria reaches for her journal, eager to write her dream down, before it escapes into light of day.

65

Prunella's Hair Salon

Grandmother Promise steeps her long silver hair in a gigantic cauldron filled to the brim with Chamomile flowers. Prunella is helping her dye her hair again by pouring the hot tea over her head, as she has done for many years. The flowers are turning Promise's silver locks into shimmering pale yellow,

'the color of butter' Prunella thinks licking her whiskers.

"Blondes do have more fun, or so they use to say," Promise crows in her raspy voice.

She loves this calming ritual of adornment, with Prunella's soft pad paws gently massaging her scalp.

"You smell divine too," purrs Prunella.

Suddenly Promise's eyes fill with tears,

"I wish my mother could be here for my birthday celebration this year. I'll be one hundred and fifty seven years old and I still miss my mama. I know how much she'd love meeting the Angels," Promise adds, smiling through her tears.

"Perhaps she is one of them," Prunella interjects.

"Prunella, that is a brilliant thought. Why didn't I think of that? What if that is true?" Promise wonders.

"We could scry and ask her," Prunella suggests.

"Yes! That is exactly what we'll do. We shall scry and ask her!"

Promise leans her head back into the cauldron, in a good mood again. Prunella grins whisker to whisker pleased with herself.

"Promise, you promised to tell me a story," she says.

"Ummm… I did, didn't I.

Promise closes her eyes, flipping through her mental Rolodex of all the stories she has told Prunella.

"Ah yes. Let's see. I think you're ready to hear this one. Or wait, perhaps this one. Well, I shall tell you both of them."

Promise begins her first story.

66

Promise's Two Creation Stories

In the beginning God was a circle. She circled round and round and round herself. Having no where to go, she finally had to admit, even if only to herself,

"I am so bored. There must be something else. Something more besides endless, infinite me."

Suddenly, God had an idea!

' I'll split myself in two. One part will be me. The other part, I'll set free. Free to watch me, adore me, worship me, penetrate me and make more of me. That part I will call He. And I will be She.'

"And that is what God did. Thank God for that. Just imagine. What if God hadn't been bored? We might not even exist."

Promise closes her eyes and goes quiet, thinking Prunella needs time to let the story settle inside her mind. But Prunella moves on to more important matters.

"What is it like to fall in love?" Prunella asks.

"Excellent question Prunella," Promise inhales deeply to begin.

"To fall in love is Sweet. To stay in love is Salty. To fall out of love is Sour. To regret having been in love is Bitter. But to never, ever love, Stinks Rotten. Better to let our heart's be broken, crushed and close down for a time, than to never have opened our heart to love. And know that with our desire to merge, to join in union with another, will also brings the pain of separation," Promise adds sadly.

Prunella laps up Promise's wisdom like cream.

"Tell me more," she purrs.

"My next story will explain it better." Promise says.

"It is just as God, our Creator felt when he let us go. God loved us like this. He loved us so much, he held on to us so tightly. He pressed us so hard against his breast, that we were suffocating, weeping in pain.

Then God saw what he was doing and so he inhaled and expanded and expanded his chest so wide. It was the Big Bang! When he exhaled He set us free. But oh, the pain was so great, none of us believed we would survive it. He inhaled again and when he exhaled we were thrown out into space in every direction. Then He blew on us, sending us even further and further into the Void.

Where are we going? We cried. It is so cold and so dark. Take us back we screamed.' But it was too late.

God inhaled one more time and only those who had held on by some miracle, remained with him. They became the Seraphim. Beings of pure Light reflecting all God's glory.

The Great Sacrifice God made was in letting go of all he loved. So that all he loved could live free of his control or possession."

Promise says, lifting her head out of the cauldron and smiling.

"Let's get my hair dry and then we'll go a scrying," she says, winking at Prunella.

67

The Scrying Bowl

Promise, Prunella, Euphoria and Glorious are gathered around the scrying bowl. They are watching Great Grandmother Sparkle's final perform at *Le Theatre Du Sapienta*.

"Sparkle was so glamorous," Euphoria sighs.

"That's who we get our talents from," Promise says proudly.

"For being such Drama Queens," Glorious adds.

"Now, let's get back to the business at hand," Promise says.

Whisking her hands over the scrying bowl to clear it, Promise inhales deeply and asks,

"Mother, what do you know about the Angels now on Earth?"

The water's surface grows very dark, as if the depths of space has poured itself into the bowl. Sparkle's face appears peering back at them. Her mouth opens wide and in place of her tongue there is a white rose with a large sparkling tear drop right in its center.

All four of them gasp in unison, as her image fades.

"What does that tell us?" Prunella asks everyone.

"My Mother was never one for giving anyone a direct answer. We Greens seem to thrive upon being obtuse," Promise chuckles.

"It's obvious. She just told us she knows about the Angel Tear Potion." Euphoria says.

"That's right. There it was plain as day in her mouth, an Angel Tear on a Rose," Glorious adds.

"Exactly. She knows," Euphoria says.

"There's another question I want to ask her, in private please," Promise requests.

Euphoria and Glorious and Prunella step away leaving Promise alone with the scrying bowl.

Promise leans in close and whispers into the water,

"Mother, are you one of the Angels here on Earth now?"

The water turns dazzling brilliant azure blue. A chorus of voices rises up and out from its depths. High, otherworldly, heavenly tones coming from a great distance, far beyond New Witch.

Intuitively Promise understands the response to her question in her heart and begins to weep into the bowl. Her tears change the water back to a reflection of her own face again.

Prunella has come back, rubbing herself against Promise's leg.

Promise looks at her, smiling sadly,

"No she's not here. Mother is not here among the Angels on Earth. She is still with God in Heaven."

68

Euphoria & Adore

"Oh how I wish you could come with me to New Witch. You'd love the Enchantment Garden," Euphoria says.

"Bring the Enchantment Garden clearly into focus in your mind and I will be able to see it."

Hearing Adore say this only makes Euphoria sadder.

"I want more of you. I want more than our telepathic ecstatic love making. I want to know what you really look like Adore." she confesses.

"Not like this. You would not recognize me," Adore admits.

"What would I see?" Euphoria asks.

"You would see me as pure light in motion. You would see me as a luminous field, contracting and expanding," Adore explains.

"I will be bereft when you leave," Euphoria says nervously.

"What makes you say I will leave?" Adore asks gently.

Adore can hear Euphoria's heart is beating very fast as she begins to tell him all about her experiments with Emeraldine's Tears.

"Adore, I have a confession to make. Several weeks ago an Angel fell into New Witch forest. I call her Emeraldine. We've become the best of friends. In our realm, she hasn't turned to stone."

"She can move and speak. She floats more than walks and bounces like a balloon when she gets excited. She laughs and weeps over everything. We have discovered that her tears have tremendous power. I've been holding back from telling you this before because I believe they will free you. And once you are free I will lose you forever." Euphoria begins to cry.

"Bring me Emeraldine's Tears." Adore says.

It is the first time Adore has ever asked for anything. Euphoria is shocked into action. She shoots up into the air and speeds back to New Witch to get them.

**

When Euphoria returns, she is holding Emeraldines Tears in a vial and her hands are shaking violently. With tears of her own streaming down her face, she asks Adore

"Where shall we start?"

"My eyes," Adore instructs her.

Euphoria places one drop of the Angel Tears in each eye. Instantaneously Adores stone hard face softens into flesh. His lips break into the most tender smile.

"My tongue," Adore says, opening his mouth.

Having only heard his voice in her mind until this moment, Adores audible voice sends Euphoria into a rapture.

She places the next drop on his tongue.

Adores chest rises. He raises his arms. His wings now almost too dazzling to behold. Euphoria is both terrified and ecstatic. Instinctively she begins dancing wildly to channel her fear and awe.

"One more drop," Adore calls out to her.

Euphoria stops dancing to place one final drop upon his tongue.

Liberated at last, his entire body springs into action. Adore reaches for Euphoria and scoops her up into his arms.

"I have something I want to show you," He says, taking flight.

Adore heads north to 72nd Street and then east to Central Park and land right smack in the very center of Strawberry Fields.

Adore sets Euphoria down. Falling to his knees, he begins weeping into the earth with total abandon. His tears are exactly like Emeraldine's. Huge, sparkling stars form in a pool around him.

Then a most amazing thing happens. Strawberry Fields begins undulating and rippling like a carpet being rolled out, with row upon row of lush flowering vegetation in rapid succession.

Adore rises taking Euphoria in his arms.

"I believe this is what you have always, truly wanted," he says.

Euphoria melts.

"Yes it is, you. I have always truly wanted you, you here with me. To share the Enchantment Garden on Earth."

"We can call it Celestial Garden. I will remain here with you Euphoria," Adore pledges.

They embrace for hours.... days actually.

69

Prunella & Mr. Right

Prunella is in the Enchantment Garden taking a Moon Bath, which she does whenever the moon is full. Sitting with her front paws perfectly straight, she makes a wish. It is the same wish she has been making since Euphoria met Adore and Emeraldine met Glorious.

"I wish an Angel would land here in New Witch especially for me. A big strong Tom cat of an Angel who'd make me his purr bride and live happily ever after with me," Prunella sighs and asks the Strawberry moon,

"What is the difference between longing and desire?" Strawberry Moon replies,

"Longing is wanting without the faith of receiving. Desire sees in faith, knowing it has already received."

Prunella grasps the idea completely, wiggling her body and grinning whisker to whisker,

"You mean, I already am a Mrs. Tom."

Suddenly there's a cry way off in the distance. Her ears perk up, scanning the air for it's location. And there it is again.

Some creature is wailing at the edge of the forest, beyond the Ancestral burial grove. Stretching, Prunella rises to follow its call.

Softly she paws the ground beneath her, warming her limbs for the journey. Making her way by the bright full moon over beds of moss and tree stumps. The are stones here are much larger than the ones she remembers along this path. Owls eyes gleaming like lanterns up in the pine branches. A chorus of toad song in the creek's silvery light.

After a while she hears the wailing sound again. This time it is much louder, somewhere close by. Perhaps up in a tree nearby. But which tree? She stops, scanning the branches above her head.

"MeeeOoow."

There it is. High above her in the branches of the ancient Red Wood tree. Prunella sees the outline of the creature up there. It has long dark wings and is clinging to the bark, with large claws.

"What kind of a bird are you?" Prunella asks it.

"I am who you choose to see," It responds.

Prunella's heart leaps in recognition. She scrambles up the tree, praying it be true. And behold, it is!

His fur is thick, lush dark purple velvet. His eyes are amethyst saucers. His wings are dark and iridescent indigo. Prunella almost swoons, but catches herself quickly. Instead she inquires in her most seductive purr cat voice,

"Are you lost?"

"Not really. It's just that I have never been a cat before. Not sure what I am supposed to do with four legs. Also my wings don't work. Not feeling very much like your hero. If you know what I mean," He says confidentially.

Prunella realizes she must take the lead and show him how a cat moves to help him get down the tree.

"No probleme", she replies in a faux Italian accent.

"I will show you how to move your legs. Just watch me."

Putting on her most seductive swagger, Prunella moves her legs in a slow, exaggerated motion, alternating left front, right back.

Angel Cat catches on quickly. Imitating Prunella, he makes it down the tree to the forest floor right behind her.

An awkward moment of silence follows.

"My name is Prunella," she says, blushing deeply violet beneath her lavender fur.

"I am who you choose to see," Angel Cat says, getting shy all over again.

Prunella barely hesitates,

"Purrfecto," she says, rolling it off her tongue dramatically.

Purrfecto smiles and nods his approval.

"Good choice," He says.

Prunella looks up at Strawberry Moon, who winks back at her.

"This way Purrfecto. This is the way back home," Prunella says, trying to conceal her excitement.

They walk side by side.

Two hearts thumping and bumping in unison.

70

Emeraldine's Secret

Angels do not bleed. Unless they have fallen into New Witch. Then the rules change. Emeraldine has just gotten her very first 'period.' She has been giggling about it for several days, but dares not tell anyone.

"I need to keep this a secret for now. It will frighten them, especially Euphoria," Emeraldine warns herself, while slicing a large piece of Shroom pie for her breakfast.

She sits down at the kitchen table, ready to devour all of its savory deliciousness of black pepper, cumin and coriander and melt in your mouth Chestnut pie crust.

Euphoria comes down to the kitchen for her morning brew. She too has a secret she is keeping from everyone, waiting for the right moment to share her BIG NEWS. Instead she decides to makes small talk.

"What is Heaven?" Euphoria asks casually.

Slowly licking pie crust crumbs from her lips, Emeraldine counters her with her own light chatter.

"What is Earth?"

"Earth is where souls go to experience living in a physical body," Euphoria replies.

Emeraldine sits straight, pulling her belly in before responding.

"Heaven is where souls live in Eternity in a Light Body. Angels on the other hand, are eternal beings of Light. We do not have souls. We exist outside of time. For us there is no day, there is no night, nor are there any seasons," Emeraldine explains.

"Oh dear, I would miss the loveliness of the seasons terribly," Euphoria protests.

"Heaven is where Life is Eternal," Emeraldine says.

"Eternal at which phase? Seed, Blossom, Fruit or Decay?"

"All phases together at the same time," Emeraldine explains.

"How is it possible?" Euphoria asks, completely perplexed.

"You will see someday, but not for a very long time."

Sneaking a date nut roll from the dessert dish, Emeraldine stuffs it into her fat cheeks before turning away from Euphoria's watchful eyes.

71

Euphoria's Class & The Angel Potion

Everyone in Euphoria's herbal class has taken the Angel Potion. Building their trust means a lot right now moving forward.

"Thank you for your courage and faith in the work we have been doing. This Potion is a life transforming experience. As you can already see, you are not the same women you were just one week ago," Euphoria says, with a glint in her eye.

All nine women begin yelping like a pack of baby wolves. Each woman is pulling a scarf off or rolling back a Tee shirt to reveal their flower. Each rose is a unique shade of Terra Red, ranging from brilliant crimson to blood orange.

One of the women stands to speak on behalf of the rest of the class. She asks the question that has been on all their minds.

"Euphoria, Please tell us, what exactly is in this Potion?"

Euphoria's face drops. She hates having to withhold information from her students, but for now she still has no other choice.

"I cannot divulge my recipe at this time. Let it suffice to say that it is a gift from Nature to us, for our evolution and the world's."

"Even if you all knew exactly what the ingredients are, it would not change anything. It is new unknown ground for all of us, including myself. I can promise you this though, I will not market or promote this Potion as a product. I will not sell it anywhere or to anyone to profit by."

The women remain quiet, absorbing and digesting her words.

"You can already feel significant changes in your perception and consciousness, correct?" Euphoria asks.

All the women nod in the affirmative.

"All I ask, is that you guard this gift well. Please continue to hide it's effect for now. Be creative about it. Have fun with it and enjoy the adventure. It is an extraordinary opportunity for us. From now on, this class is a Sisterhood of mutual support. We will travel this new road together," Euphoria declares, extending her arms as she moves among them, embracing each woman.

In turn all the women embrace one another. A bonding unison humming in their bones. They all feel it. They all know it is blooming, rippling, liberating the unifying light of truth in them.

72

Promise & Onyx Rescue Helios

Promise's one hundred and fifty-seventh birthday celebration feels incomplete. As magical as it with her strutting around Faery Cakes in a gorgeous raspberry chiffon gown, listening to all her friends take turns praising and adoring her, she cannot wait until the party is over, so she can head back downtown to share her surprise Birthday gift from Emeraldine with Onyx.

For the public's sake, Promise blows out eighty- seven candles on her Birthday cake in one breath. After serving all her guests generous slices of the sublime Triple Layer Strawberry Shortcake that Glorious baked, Promise excuses herself and goes outside to share the rest of the cake with the neighborhood children. That's when she makes her getaway, along with her Birthday gift from Emeraldine. A stunning crystal vial filled with Angel Tears.

***

Onyx listens passively to Promise, as she babbles on and on about her Birthday party. But she doesn't say a thing.

"Onyx, I am boring you?"

Onyx just rolls her eyes.

"Just go ahead and put a drop in my eye already."

Promise blushes scarlet from head to toe.

"How could I forget? You can read my mind. Of course, how foolish of me. OK, OK, just one minute."

Promise takes the crystal vial out of her velvet satchel.

"Truth be told, I am terrified. That if this works, I will lose you. Onyx, please don't fly away. Don't leave me. It will break my heart," Promise confesses.

Floating a few inches up off the roof, face to face with Onyx, Promise places one drop in each of her eyes.

Instantly Onyx's lips begin to quiver and her entire face begins to glow and soften. And for the very first time, Onyx smiles.

"More," She says with her beautiful mouth and beautiful voice.

Promise places the next drop on Onyx's tongue and stands back to watch the miracle unfold.

Onyx's entire body blooms into a beacon of female strength, ablaze with shimmering topaz wings.

Promise almost faints from the sheer colossal beauty of Onyx, who shakes her out of her stupor.

"Quick," she says, "We must leave now and get to Helios."

Onyx rises straight into the air as Promise quickly tucks the Angel Tears into her satchel. The two take to the starry night sky. Destination: The World Trade Center Station.

***

Helios has been expecting them. As they get near the station, he lets Onyx know that they should wait until more people leave.

By 3:00 am most of the people have gone home. Onyx and Promise descend upon Helios to the astonishment of a handful of onlookers.

Promise ignores their gasps and places two drops of the Angel Tears into Helios's eyes.

Nothing happens right away. Several more minutes pass, then finally the skin of mirror over Helios's face dissolves into thin air. In its place a very human face overflowing with kindness is beaming a smile with the most exquisite ruby lips you can imagine.

"More," Helios says, in a deep baritone voice that goes echoing throughout the station.

One more drop to his tongue and all the mirror flesh over his body evaporates. Helios is a magnificent warrior of light with olive skin, eyes of Amber light and hair the color of spun Gold.

"Come, let us go and help the others," he says.

And off they go, leaving a stunned group of people behind ready to tell the tale on the Morning News.

***

Jade and Pearl are having breakfast while watching the morning news. A video taken at the World Trade Center Station comes on. There without a doubt, is none other than Promise Green, still in her Birthday gown of Raspberry Chiffon, flying off with two other Angels. Jade and Pearl are somewhat shocked and confused to say the least. Later that afternoon, they confront Euphoria.

"You never told us your Grandmother is an Angel."

"Well," Euphoria swallows and grins, "Not exactly."

73

The After Glow

Helios and Onyx and Promise continue liberating the Angels on Earth. Euphoria and Adore are busy creating Celestial Gardens all over Manhattan Isle, the Bronx, Brooklyn, Queens and Staten Island.

It is of no surprise to anyone, that many of the liberated Angels also choose to remain on Earth to help activate higher consciousness in the people.

Gradually news of the miraculous Celestial Garden ignites an over whelming demand for its replication across the entire planet. Literally nourishing the masses of humanity who have dared to dream the restoring of Earth to its original glory. Finally everyone can see what is possible and are eager and ready to step up and do their part.

The infusion of plant kingdom consciousness within the human species has triggered an evolutionary leap. The Angel Tear Rose Potion has birthed a new kind of human. They choose to call themselves the Flower People.

As Flower People they still have the option to continue to eat for the pleasure it gives them. Sharing meals together with family and friends is valued. And they are also capable of receiving complete sustenance directly from the Sun and Soil and Rain. Humanity's destiny is to live abundantly with all organic sentient souls.

***

Jade is carefully pulling a thin strip of bees wax off of her client's tattoo. She has recently started infusing Bee Propolis into her ink and sealing it with Bees Wax to dry. The result is stunning. The tattoo looks as if it is embossed in velvet.

As a finishing touch, Jade rubs on a luscious lotion she's made with Ruby Gem Stone Honey, rose water, orange oil & clove oil.

Her client Florenza moans with pleasure inhaling the lotion's heavenly fragrance. She stands up and looks down at the new tattoo shimmering above her ankle. Throwing her arms around Jade,

"Muchas muchas, Gracias," She says.

Florenza is a glorious example of a Flower Person. Scantily clad, well heeled and magnificently bejeweled in Potion flowers.

"Who needs make-up? Or designer clothes?" Florenza says, laughing out the door, blowing kisses to Jade.

***

Soon there will be Flower People everywhere, openly flaunting their flowery selves on the streets of every city and town. Young and old sporting their favorite blooms at work, at play and at home with family and friends.

Some may chose to sprout full body micro gardens, to attract and feed Bees, Butterflies and Hummingbirds.

It's a new day in Paradise!

74

Emeraldine's Big Secret

This morning Bella and Prunella have been collaborating with Emeraldine on ideas for the baby's nursery.

Emeraldine has asked them to keep her pregnancy a secret, until she figures out how to tell Glorious herself first.

"How was I to know kissing would lead to conception?" Emeraldine says, feigning her innocence.

"No one conceives by kissing alone," Prunella chides.

Emeraldine blushes deep violet.

"Well of course we did more than kiss," she admits.

"He swept me off my feet with that glorious mouth of his. I melted on the spot. Desire engulfed us. We were consumed in its flames. We dissolved in blissful union, soared on high to infinite peaks of ecstasy." She says, swaying as she recalls their passion.

"As you can see, I'm really glad it happened," placing her palms on her belly swelling under the pale blue silk robe Bella borrowed from Promise and discreetly gifted her to hide her blessing with.

"What worries me now is what if our baby has wings? Glorious has never liked mine," Emeraldine says pouting.

"I doubt your baby will have wings. Witchess fly without them," Prunella assures her.

"That is so true. Oh Prunella, you are going to make a fantastic Auntie Cat to Baby Crystalline," she says lovingly stroking Prunella's favorite spot under her chin.

75

Wedding Bells

"I love my whole body and everyone in it!" Emeraldine declares, feeling her baby moving inside her. Her bouncy walk has transformed into a kind of ballet. She is all Pirouettes and Grand Plies.

She goes twirling about the kitchen, baking Cherry pies for Glorious and Blueberry Cup Cakes for Baby Crystalline, because eating for two is definitely twice the fun.

Telling Glorious wasn't as scary as Emeraldine had thought it would be. His response was gloriously unexpected. He did several cart wheels, howled ' Victory 'and went down on one knee asking Emeraldine to marry him.

Loving Emeraldine has transformed Glorious as well. It has given him a new understanding of himself. A contentment and confidence that show up in his voice, now flowing with richer resonance and sonorous cadences. Everyone can feel the intense pleasure he has enunciating "my wife" and "our baby."

Bella is absolutely beside herself with joy, in preparation for the wedding. Ransacking the Ancestors wardrobe for authentic fashions since Emeraldine told her she wants a 1960's theme wedding.

Witch Hazel wants The Beatles " All You Need Is Love " to be played instead of Here Comes the Bride as she walks Emeraldine down the aisle in the Enchantment Garden.

Emeraldine has her heart set on a white paper mini dress for a wedding gown. How to accomplish her bridal vision, given her belly's bloom, leaves Bella with some truly imaginative work ahead of her. Flowered bell bottoms and white ruffled shirt for Glorious. Bold floral maxi dress and rhinestone slippers for Promise.

Prunella, a natural pick for flower girl, requests white go-go boots. And Purrfecto, as ring bearer, in just a Peter Max print tie.

Witch Hazel, on the other hand, insists Bella make her a dress entirely out of moss. She wants something earthy and noble, perhaps a few Star Bee volunteers adding points of light to the neck line, sleeves and hem.

Euphoria, as one would expect, continues being mysterious, telling everyone she hasn't decided what she'll be wearing just yet.

She will surprise them.

76

More After Glow

Bliss Alley is going strong. Allure's allure bringing in a steady flow of people eager to slip into Tantric bliss. There are more taxis cruising by this block than ever before, ready to pick up people departing the shrine, who dare not ride public transportation after their session for fear of breaking the heavenly spell.

***

Emeraldine smiles and fans herself with the sheet of paper she is writing on. It is a new recipe on for the Angel Tears that Jade & Pearl will be taking on their trip cross country this summer to personally introduce people to the Potion.

Although Emeraldine has yet to meet Jade and Pearl in person, she feels a bond of Sisterhood between them.

***

Euphoria and Adore remain on Manhattan Isle help cultivating hybrid consciousness that has now been fully activated among all the plants, minerals, insects and animals living within Celestial Gardens. These gardens are a public sanctuary for all people to come to share and learn, communing with Nature as a community at a level never known before.

The Angels on Earth continue raising consciousness for the masses, who are still discovering and learning while gathering at their feet in towns and cities all over the world.

There is no shortage of Angel Tears. A gift from the God, free, and plentifully abundant, as long as humans choose them to be.

Let Us Pray.

77

Witch Hazel Is Thinking

Witch Hazel is sewing crystals on Emeraldine's wedding veil. Already envisioning the sunlight sparkling on them as she walks down the aisle with Emeraldine on her wedding day.

Her mind begins swirling, formulating conclusions to the events on Earth since the Angels arrival.

"The poisoning of the Earth finally reached Heaven itself. The Angels fell to Earth to awaken in people new possibilities.

They held everyone in their grasp without fear or aggression. Without force or manipulation, or the exchange of money.

Their presence here has led to the revelation of human spirit and consciousness, demonstrating humanity's innate predisposition to caring, creativity and truth.

A testament to our Creator's miraculous love for our purpose in the universe. Now the Angel Tears Potion will assist humanity restore the light and balance across this planet as it never has been seen before."

78

Scrying Again

Promise, Prunella and Witch Hazel go scrying again.
"There is something going on with Euphoria. It's not like me to meddle in her affairs, but I can't resist taking a peak!"

Prunella and Witch Hazel both start laughing,

"Go on Promise," Witch Hazel teases. "Let's all have a look."

Promise moves her hands over the bowl in a clockwise direction, looking into the future.

The water in the bowl begins to sparkle, turning cerulean blue with twinkling with silver stars. Two tiny faces appear side by side. One face has bright green eyes with pale blue hair. The other face has golden eyes with raven black hair.

"Oh my goodness!" Promise gasps.

"What did I tell you," Prunella whispers to Witch Hazel.

Bella slides two carved wooden cradles across the floor, almost knocking the scrying bowl over. A note is fluttering between them.

For Baby Crystalline & Baby Estrella Luz
All My Love, Your Godmother
Casa Bella

79

After Euphoria

When one has seen Manhattan Isle's entire evolution, from its infancy as a supreme paradise of pristine woodlands, lakes and streams, to its present condition, it is easy to despair.

Euphoria carries a cord of pearls belonging to her mother, Peace Green. She feels the movement of life inside her womb.

Already it senses her thoughts and her feelings.

"These pearls will belong to you someday Estrella Luz. And while our ancestors weeping did nothing to stop other forces from devouring what it wanted. In spite of that, God's love continues dancing in our homes and work places. Water runs through pipes. Earth transforms into glass. Fossils into fuel. Air breathes into our furnaces and cooling devices. Fire dances in the electric lines.

We are living in a Light World.

Where do we go from here? What will we become?"

Euphoria hears her baby reply,

    " *We Are Who We Choose To See* "

Acknowledgments

Not one word of this book could have been written without the infinite beauty, grace and intelligence of Nature.

And, if not for the loving support of my extraordinary friends, these pages would have remained in a closet and not here, printed and bound into a book. I am blessed beyond words for you all.

Teresa Hammack, Thank you my precious friend! You brought such a fierce light to my writing process. As my first reader, your response was everything I had hoped for and so much more.

Tarleton Stone, Thank you for inspiring and igniting the flame that became this story. You are a miraculous, brilliant light in my life.

Patrice Tappe, For being the extraordinary talented friend, teacher and generous human being you are. Thank you for sharing your artistic eye for detail to my first draft. Your suggestions and corrections have made this a better book in every way.

Carol Loomis, Thank you for pouring your delicious enthusiasm all over my first draft. It was the much needed wind beneath my wings.

Trey Zimmerman, Thank you for reading my second draft with Holy Spirit X-Ray Vision eyes. Your encouraging words helped launch the rocket of faith needed to getting this book out into the world.

Author's Notes

Dear Readers,
The songs from this book are available on my website.
The Music of Angels and Witchess
www.robertabaum.com

www.ingramcontent.com/pod-product-compliance
Lightning Source LLC
LaVergne TN
LVHW020430070526
838199LV00025B/585/J